The Shallows

Nigel Bird

A Sea Minor Publication

Copyright © 2016 Nigel Bird
All rights reserved.

ISBN-13:
978-1530225156

ISBN-10:
1530225159

Also by Nigel Bird
Southsiders: That's Alright
Mr Suit
Dirty Old Town (and other stories)
Beat On The Brat (and other stories)
With Love And Squalor
How To Choose A Sweetheart
Smoke
In Loco Parentis

Nigel's work also appears in:
Speedloader
True Brit Grit
Grimm Tales
Pulp Ink
Mammoth Best British Crime 8
Mammoth Best British Crime 9
Protectors
Both Barrels

To Fiona Waddell for all her kindness and support.
Here's to the Great Escape. May your world remain forever purple

The Shallows
one

"What's the matter Dad?" Shem's rod shook over the water as the sun dropped behind the hills. The loch had turned the colour of black ink.

"I'm fine." He wasn't. He was a man of habits and routines. The changes he was about to put his family through were making his head spin.

"You shouldn't worry about me, Dad. I didn't like the school much and I'll make friends before you or Mum, you'll see."

Brad was proud of his boy. "I know you will, Shem. You getting any interest?"

"Not even a tickle."

"Then let's call it a night."

"No way." His thin seven-year old arms and legs were covered in goose-bumps and he still wasn't ready to go home. "Mum's looking forward to frying up fresh trout."

"That might be what she said, but she hates taking the guts out and she can't cook them for toffee. I reckon she'll be happy with another trip into town."

"Chinese?"

"Whatever you fancy. Let's pack up and leave before those storm-clouds burst."

*

Brad wiped away the mist from the windscreen with his forearm and turned on the radio. The sounds of violins from Classic FM mingled with the gentle tapping of the rain. He turned the volume down so as not to disturb Shem who was asleep in the tent.

Molly sipped her beer and put her feet up on the dash. She drew a stick man with a big sad face on her window. "You still feel like this, Honey?"

"I guess."

Molly took his hand and stroked the back of it with her thumb. "Thinking about Richardson again?"

He nodded.

"Well don't. It wasn't your fault. There was nothing you could do."

"Maybe."

"There's no maybe about it. You're a good man. You did all you were able." She added tears to her sketch with the tip of her finger. "That's all we can ever do. It's what you tell Shem all the time."

"I suppose. If I could erase his face from my memory I'd be okay. Every time I close my eyes, he's there." He pictured him in uniform, his hands shaking and the tears rolling down his cheeks.

Molly looked at her watch.

"Time is it?"

"Half past ten. You can still return if you want. Just tell them it was the traffic or the weather or something. They'll let you off with a warning and it will all be forgotten."

The muscles in Brad's neck tightened. "I told you, I'm never going back." The plan was in place and he wasn't about to change his mind. "As soon as I walk through those gates I'm theirs. It won't be long until they send me away for another ninety days. When I see Shem again, he'll have grown a couple of inches and he'll have a million new stories to tell." He hated that his son growing up without him. It wasn't right. "When we have the next one, I want to be there for each of the stages."

A downpour thrashed the car. It sounded like the end of the world. Drops bounced high off the bonnet. Bach's sonata disappeared in the pounding. Molly squeezed Brad's hand and leant over and kissed him on the cheek. She drew a new face on his window. This time, the mouth turned up in a smile.

"That supposed to make me feel better?"

"No," Molly told him. "This is what'll do that." She planted her lips on his. He let the soft heat warm his spirits and distract him from his Faslane nightmares. Her tongue entered his mouth and it was game over. She unbuttoned his shirt, scratched his chest hair, slid her hand over his money belt and stopped at the top of his jeans.

"Mum! Dad!" Shem's shouting was barely audible, but both of them heard it.

"Damn it." Molly sat back in the passenger seat and folded her arms.

"My turn. You stay where you are." Brad opened the door and stepped into a puddle. Paused to admire his wife. Her tanned legs stretched out from her denim shorts and the tie in her shirt showed enough of her midriff to remind him of what fine shape she was in. When he got back, he would kiss every inch of her. "I'll be quick."

"Dad!" Shem's voice was louder now. "Quick. The tent's flooding."

Brad swore under his breath. The tent was brand new. Top of the range. Guaranteed for just about everything the British weather might throw at it. The guy at the store said you could pitch it at the bottom of the sea and stay dry. Brad suppressed the urge to go back there and smack that smile from the salesman's face. He unzipped the awning door and entered. Shem stood there in the communal compartment between the bedrooms. The sleeping-bag he wore pulled up to his chin was soaked.

"Show me where it's coming from." He picked up the torch from the folding table and went through.

"It's leaking in from the side." Shem's teeth chattered as he spoke. "It woke me up."

In Shem's room, the groundsheet was flooded. His story books and clothes were sodden. "That's some mess you've got in there. I wonder if ours is any better." He unzipped the door of the double and searched it with the beam of his light. Things weren't as bad. One of the roll mats was still dry and the cases were safe. Molly's bed hadn't fared so well. It was right beneath a steady drip.

"Can we sleep in the car Dad?" Trust Shem to see this as a big adventure. "We'll share the dry bag and cuddle up in the back seat."

It was a good idea, except it would be cold and cramped in there. Brad was sick of being confined. Life on the submarine had him craving open spaces and clean air. Being suffocated within another metal box didn't appeal. "If we must. First off, we'll check out that building we saw when we drove down. Grab anything that's dry and we'll shove it in the boot. And don't forget your glasses."

If the old barn proved adequate, they could hang around for a few days. Let the dust settle and give them space to breathe before setting off for their new lives.

two

Captain Shanks knocked on the door, stepped in and saluted.

Commander Briggs removed his feet from the desk, closed the paperback he was reading and took the empty pipe from his mouth. The lines around his eyes made themselves known as he smiled. "Sit down Shanks. Tell me what I can do for you."

Shanks removed the pile of papers from the chair and sat down. Unsure of where to leave the forms, he kept them on his lap. "We've got a no show sir."

Briggs put the pipe into his mouth and chewed the stem. "Enlighten me."

"It's one of Blue Watch. Lieutenant Bradley Heap. He was due back this evening at nineteen hundred hours. We've not heard a thing."

"Heap? He's been with us quite a while now."

"Five years."

"Practically a veteran. Nice guy. Has he ever failed to turn up before?"

"Never."

"Any blots on the copybook?"

"Not since training."

Briggs swatted the air and stood. "Then there's nothing to worry about."

Shanks cleared his throat. "You're probably right. I only brought this along because of the Richardson incident."

"Ah." Briggs set off pacing in the way he always did when things were complicated. "Remind me."

"Three weeks ago, when Blue Watch was on the way home, there was an issue involving Midshipman Richardson." Shanks turned his head to follow his commander. "Something of a sexual nature from what we can establish."

"I remember."

"Whatever it was, Richardson felt the need to unburden himself to the counsellor."

"Who was Bradley Heap, as I recall."

"Correct."

"Am I also right in thinking that Heap's words of wisdom weren't up to the job?"

"I'm not sure we can say that exactly. He noted everything down and logged his concern with the Commanding Officer."

"Except it made no difference."

"Richardson took an overdose. They found him dead in his bunk when they went to wake him for his shift."

"What a shame. They're finding it difficult to find suitable recruits these days. Men with spine is what we need. A tougher induction process would do the trick." Briggs sat again. Sucked on his pipe as if he were smoking. "I hear he almost forced the early return of the vessel."

"The captain was faced with a tough decision."

"Didn't they keep him in the torpedo tubes?"

"I think there was space in the freezer, sir."

"And you suspect that our Bradley Heap isn't coping with the situation."

"It's possible." Shanks crossed his legs and dropped some of the papers. He bent down and picked them up. "Heap was debriefed when they disembarked. The doc gave him the all-clear."

"Then what exactly is the problem?"

Shanks straightened his spine. Wondered if the whole situation wasn't just a vivid creation of his idle mind. "I don't like this one. All those whistle-blowers wanting to make the world a better place make me nervous. We're talking about sex and suicide on Trident submarines, sir. You can imagine the lefties having a field day if Heap decided to cause a stir."

Briggs raised his eyebrows higher than should have been possible. Nodded his head. "I see what you mean. But let's not get this out of proportion. You follow the usual procedures and I'll make a note of your visit. If Heap's not back by breakfast, you'll have my permission to unleash your dogs."

"Thank you."

"Will that be all?"

"Yes sir." Shanks got up. He returned the pile of papers to the seat, stood tall and saluted. The bad feeling he had when he reported to the office still clung to him like bonfire smoke.

three

Shem was asleep on the back seat by the time they pulled up outside the building. It was a farmstead ripe for renovation. A small cottage stood to the right with a long block of stables running from it. To the left was a barn which jutted out at the rear. A corrugated roof provided a sheltered area in the L-shape of the walls. For now, all that was being kept dry were a rusted-beyond-repair flatbed, a pile of assorted scrap metal and a forest of thistles. The windows out back had been boarded up. While there were people homeless in the world, it was such a ridiculous waste.

Molly and Brad got out of the car and ran for cover.

The door was open. Brad put his hand through and felt about until he found a light switch. He pressed it and the room lit up before them.

"You're a genius." Molly wrapped her arms round Brad's neck and kissed him hard. "That beard of yours looks sexier every day. You should run away more often."

Brad scratched his face at the mention. "I suppose I'll get used to it."

"It makes me horny." She stroked his stubble. "Now, where were we when Shem interrupted us earlier?" She walked over to the table in the middle of the room and pressed hard to test it. "This'll do." She removed her coat, untied the knot in her shirt and held out her hand for Brad. He took it and allowed her to reel him in. His hands wandered over her breasts and his body filled with charge. She unbuttoned his trousers while he nibbled at her neck and fondled her tight buttocks. She unclipped his money belt and let it fall to the ground. Brad's hormones were rampant. He gasped as she took hold of him and slipped him inside.

*

It didn't take long for them to complete their unfinished business. The pair collapsed into each other laughing and panting. With Molly, sex was so much fun.

When Brad caught his breath, he held her close and examined the potential of the place as home for a night or two. "Isn't it awesome? Imagine owning it and letting it getting into this mess."

There was a Belfast sink in the corner and a rusty stove to the side. The wall between the rooms had collapsed, as had the staircase and parts of the ceiling.

"It's a crying shame." Molly pulled up her shorts and tied up her shirt. Her face flushed even though there was a chill in the air. "Imagine what we could do to it. You think it's safe?"

Brad went over to the fireplace and pushed the mantelpiece and the walls. "Seems solid enough." He walked through into the back and saw a door that stood out from everything else. It was new. Its shiny steel radiated heat. He warmed his hands there for a moment. "Looks like we've landed on our feet." They could hang out their equipment to dry while they rested up.

Molly came over. Touched it with her fingertips. Smiled. "Think you can get in?"

If whoever had been there last had fixed the padlock, it might not have been possible. They hadn't. He lifted it out and dropped it to the floor. Slid the bolt back and pulled the handle.

"Wait." Molly touched his arm. "Maybe there's something spooky on the other side. Aliens or mad dogs."

"Aye, right." He pushed it open.

Bright light and humid air poured from the room. The smell of herbs was overwhelming. There were green plants everywhere. It reminded him of the tropical rooms at the botanic gardens.

"Jesus." Molly put her hands to her mouth. They weren't big enough to hide her grin. "It's still a working farm. Feast your eyes on all this grass." She walked along a corridor running her fingers through the cannabis leaves like an excited child. "You wouldn't know a thing from the outside. The clever sods."

The Shallows

Brad tried to work out how they'd kept their work under wraps. All the windows were boarded up and lined with plastic sheeting. At the back was an enormous air filter with a long tube feeding into a built-in flue. There were water sprinklers above the rows of plants, interconnected by lengths of hose. Along the partitions, mirrors reflected the electric light to intensify the brightness. It was magnificent.

Molly went over to the nursery section. "All these babies. Aren't they cute?" She bent to get a closer look. Brad admired her thighs.

"Must cost a fortune to keep this place going."

"They wouldn't do it if they couldn't make a profit."

"There must be a million pounds worth of dope here just now."

"More than that. See all the stuff they've got bagged?"

There were twenty or so storage boxes in a line, each stuffed full with packaged gear. Brad couldn't resist. He went over to one of them, took out a bag and tore a hole. Inside was a sweet-smelling bud, sticky to the touch. He licked his fingers and savoured the taste. "I've not smoked a joint since I was sixteen."

"You mean none of your sailor friends get stoned?"

"They get stoned all right. I just don't join them."

"Well I get high sometimes when you're away. Me and the girls get together and watch films."

The hairs on the back of Brad's neck prickled and his shoulders knotted tight. He had an inkling that Molly and her friends took things too far when he was sailing. His fists clenched tight. He wanted to hit something and break it.

Molly must have sensed his anxiety. She stepped over. Turned him round. Dug her thumbs into his muscles and massaged him the way he liked. "It takes the edge off. We all miss you when you're under the sea. No phone calls or messages. You might as well be dead. So we let our hair down. No big deal. We're in it together, you know that."

He did, too. The women had it almost as tough as the men.

"Don't suppose you fancy a smoke?" Molly's eyes were shining.

"Wouldn't matter if I did. We've no papers or tobacco to roll one."

"Oh yes we do." Molly pointed into a room away from the plantation. "They've got everything we need over there."

She was right. And there was plenty more besides.

Whoever did the work must have lived on site. There was a microwave, a small gas stove and a kettle. Two beds were set up to the side, the blankets dirty and crumpled. The sink was piled high and there was an overspill of plates and mugs queuing up to be washed. Empty beer bottles littered the floor along with chocolate wrappers and packets of biscuits. There were lots of ashtrays, each overflowing with butts and half-smoked joints. An open electricity meter in a cupboard contained so many cables it looked like a plate of plastic spaghetti. It was a death trap, but it explained why the growers weren't so bothered about wasting energy.

On the little fold-up table in the middle of the room was the gear Molly had seen. There were also two handguns of a kind that Brad couldn't identify.

"Let's pass on the smoke and leave, Mol. If the three bears come home and see us eating their porridge, I'm not sure Goldilocks will get out of here in one piece."

"Where's your sense of adventure? This is the most exciting night we've had since Shem was born."

"Even though I'm a runaway and there are probably navy police after me as we speak."

"You know what I mean. Don't spoil the moment. Let's hang around and assess the situation."

Brad had done that already. A warehouse full of drugs and guns meant only one thing. Gangsters. And gangsters spelled trouble. His instinct was to run now and to think later. At least they'd be alive to tell the tale.

"It could be this is our lucky day." Molly sat down on the edge of a bed. "We could dump all the camping gear in the bushes and fill the boot with crop. Who knows how much that's worth? We pay thirty quid for a quarter ounce. You'd get a hundred batches from one of those bags alone. Think about it. We leave here with half of a million's worth of dope and it'll be so much easier to get away. They'll never find you with all that money to hide behind."

Brad rubbed his temples. "You know any dealers with that kind of cash?"

"Well no, but..."

"Exactly." His energy levels dropped. "And you think the guys who live here are just going to let us walk out with their business? It's why they have the guns, Mol. To kill people who want to play Robin Hood."

She picked up one of the guns. Changed her grip until she balanced the weight. Looked down the barrel and smiled. "Feel the power." She stepped back. Pointed it at Brad. "While we think about this a little longer, get rolling that spliff before I turn your brains into a tablecloth."

It wasn't the first time a gun had been pointed in Brad's face. It wasn't even the hundred-and-first. Even so, his stomach swelled at the sight of his wife with a weapon in her hands. He went through the drill. Deep breath. Take control of the fear. Focus on the situation. Whipped out his hand and grabbed Molly by the wrist. "Not funny." He spoke through gritted teeth. "Don't ever do anything like that again." He relaxed his jaw. "Please."

Molly looked hurt. She put the pistol back on the table. "You could still roll a smoke, couldn't you? It looks like we both need a hit."

Brad pulled over the pack of Silk Cut. Opened the lid and found two cigarettes. He took one out, licked along the join and tore it. He swept the king-size Rizla towards him and emptied out the tobacco. It may have been twelve years since he'd last done this, but his physical memory was impeccable.

Grumbling tyres on loose stones interrupted things. The pair froze and listened. A car approached, its engine getting louder all the time.

"Shem!" Molly looked frightened.

"It's okay. It'll be a couple of young lovers come to find some privacy. You stay here. I'll go and explain why we're here and we can get on our way."

"Be careful, Brad." Molly walked across and squeezed him tight. "I've only just got you back from the navy. I don't want to lose you all over again."

He kissed her forehead. "There's nothing to worry about. I've been trained for so many situations I can't imagine anything taking me by surprise." He let her go and left the building.

After the heat of the hot-house, the air was freezing. His eyes took a while to grow accustomed to the darkness. It was like coming off a tour on the sub and finding his depth perception out of synch. He stood and waited for the blurred shapes to come into focus.

Parked in front of his own Volvo estate was a brand new Range Rover. Stepping out of it, two big men. They definitely weren't teenagers looking for a quiet place to get it on. The driver wore black. There was a slight shine to his leather jacket. He was tall and powerfully built. His silver-grey crew cut suggested military. "What the hell are you doing here?" The voice rumbled. Its deep tones made Brad feel inadequate.

"The man asked you a question." The passenger carried his weight in a spare tyre around his belly. His black fringe was greasy and stuck to his spotty forehead. Brad reckoned him to be Chinese. Not that his nationality was important. What mattered was that he was holding a semi-automatic machine gun and didn't look the type to pause for thought before pulling the trigger.

The pair walked to the front of their vehicle and came together.

The Shallows

"Hi." It was time to settle things down. Remove the confrontation. "We were just looking for a place to sleep. My boy's over there in the car. Our tent got washed out in the storm." He fingered the crucifix that hung around his neck. Remembered that God's love had deserted him of late.

"You realise you're trespassing on private property?" The driver.

"I did not." There were no signs anywhere to say so.

"When did you arrive?"

"A couple of minutes before you."

"And you've been inside?"

"The door was open."

The driver turned his head to the passenger. Slapped him hard across the cheek.

"Sorry Junior. I thought I'd locked up."

Brad took stock of the situation. These guys were in charge of a huge illegal operation. They weren't happy that their work had been discovered. They carried guns and didn't look afraid to use them. He wondered what his chances of taking them out in a fight might be. One, he thought he could cope with. The pair, he wasn't so sure. Best thing he could do was apologise and get him and his family the hell out of there. "I'm sorry. I had no idea this was private land. I'll just drive away and pretend I've seen nothing. You'll never hear from me again. Promise."

"What do you mean, seen nothing? Have you been poking around?"

The back door of the Volvo opened and Shem's sleepy head poked out. "Are we there yet Dad?"

"We'll not be staying, son. Just get yourself to sleep and we'll find somewhere else to spend the night."

The Chinese guy slipped his gun out of sight from the boy. If there was a time to let fly, this was it. Brad centred himself. Made sure he spread his weight evenly between his feet. Prepared to spring into action.

Shem looked at the strange men and then back at his dad. "Where's Mum?"

The words brought the Chinese man to attention. He lifted his weapon and pointed it straight at Brad's gut. "Your woman's here? Hear that?"

Junior clearly had. He grabbed Brad by the arm and lifted him from the ground. "You better tell me..."

There was an almighty crack in the air. A splatter of warm liquid hit Brad in the face. Everything stopped for a moment. Brad looked at the driver. There was a large dark hole where his cheek used to be. His expression was one of complete surprise. His sentence remained unfinished. He wobbled. Brad's feet returned to earth as the dead man let him go and collapsed.

The Chinese guy appeared confused. He pointed his gun at Molly and back at Brad, then turned around and ran. Three blasts from Molly and the escaping figure screamed and fell to his knees.

Shem put his fingers in his ears and cried. Brad went over and held him tight. "You wait here nice and quiet. I need to talk to your mum for a minute. Don't worry about a thing. It's just a bad dream." He laid his son on the back seat, closed the door and returned to his wife. "What were you thinking, Mol? What got into you?"

Her shooting arm dropped to her side, but she kept hold of the gun. "I thought they were going to kill you. And Shem. Because of the drugs. There's no way I could let them do that." Tears filled her eyes and spilled out onto her face. "I love you Brad. I don't want to live without you. I had to do it. You must understand."

He did. It hadn't been so long ago that he'd half-killed a guy for cycling into Shem even though it was completely Shem's fault. Brad knew that he'd have done the same as Molly if it came to protecting his son. He'd use everything at his disposal to make sure his family stayed safe. He wiped Molly's tears away and kissed her on the nose.

From back up the drive, the moans of the Chinese guy. "He's alive, Brad. I should finish him off."

Brad put out his arm and blocked her way. "That wouldn't be right. Protecting Shem's one thing. Killing a man while he's lying in the road would just be cold-blooded murder."

"So what do we do?"

"We get into the car. I drive for a while and call an ambulance. I need to bin the phone, so I might as well do a good turn with it before I chuck it out. We'll head to your Aunt's caravan the way we'd intended and carry on with life just like we planned."

"Then let's grab some dope before we go."

"Don't be daft. In a few days, my letters will arrive at the newspaper offices. The navy police will be on our trail and that's plenty. Adding an angry drugs cartel to the list of pursuers wouldn't be doing us any favours."

"I guess you're right."

"I know I am." Brad walked Molly to the car. She got in, clicked her safety belt and shut the door.

Brad turned the key in the ignition and switched the lights on. He made a three-point turn. As he drove away, the beams lit up the two bodies lying on the floor. He looked into the mirror and saw that Shem was already asleep. "Get the phone, will you?"

Molly dug around in the glove compartment for a while. She took out the phone and gazed up at the night sky.

"What you thinking?"

She smiled at him. Dialled in the numbers. "It's a shame we never got round to rolling that smoke. I reckon we both need something to keep us straight after that."

"We'll have a beer as soon as we stop."

"Here, it's ringing."

Brad took the phone. Someone answered. "Which service do you require?"

He resisted the temptation to ask what they had. Told them everything they needed to know and hung up.

four

Inspector John Locke was unimpressed at having to get out of his bed in the early hours. It was wet and cold outside and all he wanted was to pull the blankets over his head and sleep until the sun rose.

As he drove towards the crime scene, his sciatic nerve felt every bump and contour of the track. The pain stabbed at his calf. It got so bad he thought he heard his pension calling. And, by Christ, he'd earned every penny of it. There was enough in the pot for him to live well. If he ever ran out, he could get a job on the checkout at Asda. There were worse ways to make ends meet. Solving murders came top of the list.

Everything was as it should be when he arrived. There were the guys in plastic suits wandering around like astronauts. Yellow and black tape cordoned the area off into sections. Bright lights shone down from the roof of a van. A rumbling generator provided the only noise and there was a dead body slumped next to a nice looking Range Rover.

The farm building was swarming with officers. A large patch of blood stained the pebbles and dirt twenty metres away. The air stank of cannabis. A photographer capturing the scene for posterity flashed away in the background.

Ignatius Palmer poked and prodded at the corpse while chewing hard on a piece of gum.

A young man came to greet Locke. The new face on the block. Attended the conference the week before in Glasgow, the one where Locke realised just how little energy he had left for the game. The man offered his hand. "John. Nice to see you again."

Locke couldn't put a name to the face, that of a clean-cut schoolboy from one of the posh schools. The writing on the ID he wore over his waterproofs was too small to reveal anything. "You too." Locke would get a better look at the badge later. Pretend he'd known it all along. "Shame about the circumstances."

"Indeed it is."

"So what are we looking at?"

"We've got an unidentified body. The coroner's with him just now. We don't really need him to tell us that the guy received a bullet through the head or that it was within the last couple of hours." The young man pointed along the track. "Another victim was shot in the back. 999 took a call. According to the paramedics, they were only just in time to keep him alive. They rushed him off to the hospital and if we're lucky we'll get the chance to interview him."

"We've a number for the call?"

"I've got someone working on that."

"And the plates on the Rover?"

"On their way."

"Anything significant about the building?"

"That's a bonus for our team, sir. It's chock full of plants. There's enough gear in there to soothe the UK's arthritis sufferers for the next ten years."

The detective made a note of the United Kingdom reference. Put the guy in the camp of no- voters during the independence referendum. Another tosser for the blacklist.

The officer turned towards the barn and Locke managed to get a good look at the ID. "Is there anything else you need to tell me while you're here Sergeant Hawley?" He was damned if he was going to call the kid Brian.

"Not that I can think of. I'll be over in the stables when you need me. If nothing else, it's warm and dry in there. There's a flask of coffee if you fancy."

"Thanks sergeant. I'll keep that in mind." Locke turned and walked over to the body. As he got to the tape, he took out a pair of plastic overshoes and slipped them over his Doctor Marten boots.

"Ah, John. The pleasure's all yours I'm afraid."

"Don't flatter yourself."

"Now, now darling. Don't take it to heart. It's nothing personal."

"It's always personal, Ignatius."

"Did we disturb you from a hot date or something?"

"Yeah. With a feather pillow and an expensive slab of memory foam."

"You're clearly not getting enough."

"I'm not getting any."

"That's hardly surprising. Your face would turn milk sour."

"Enough of the flattery already."

"You should take a leaf out of Sergeant Hawley's book. There's someone who knows how to look after his skin. Rather dishy, don't you think?"

"No I bloody well don't. Tell me what we've got and let's get this finished."

Ignatius smiled. He took off his spectacles and wiped them onto his shirt. "There's not much you couldn't work out for yourself. There's a gunshot wound to the face. The exit point is just above the ear on the other side of the skull. He lost some of whatever brains he had over on the bonnet of the car." He pointed over at the blood and fluid with his glasses and then put them back on. "I'm supposed to draw around it, but it would be a shame to spoil such fine paintwork. I can't say for certain, but my guess is that the weapon was a small handgun similar to the one they found inside. That piece hasn't been discharged, so we can rule it out of the equation."

"Time?"

"Eleven o'clock would be near enough. The medics received the call at quarter past."

Locke put out his foot and rested the plastic cover against the victim's ear. "May I?"

"I'll not tell anyone."

Locke slipped his toe under the skull and pushed it up until he could see the face. He recognised the hard stare immediately. "Well, well, well. Sammy Davis. Also known as Junior."

"Rather unoriginally at that."

"Fancy him showing up in this neck of the woods."

"You're sure it's him?"

"Nailed on."

"That's fantastic. It'll save the team a tonne of work."

"Last I heard he was working for Red Fenton."

"Muscle or brains?"

"A bit of both." Locke flicked through his memory. Junior was a nasty type, but he was a funny guy. It was hard not to like someone with such a morbid sense of humour. "Could turn his hand to anything and probably did."

"I'm sure you're looking forward to a meeting with our Mr Fenton already. As long as he's still in the country."

Locke checked his watch. "It's a bit early in the year for him to be at the Spanish villa. I'll catch him in sunny Eyemouth."

"You get to visit the most exotic locations." Ignatius stood and stretched his back. "I'm almost jealous. Now if there's nothing else, I'm done. I'll work on your mate tomorrow. In the meantime, I'm off to reacquaint myself with a hot water bottle."

"Lucky sod." Locke nodded his farewell and walked over to the buildings.

He ducked his head and entered through the main door. The room was pleasantly warm and dry in spite of being totally derelict.

"This way John." The sergeant. If he kept up with the first name thing, he'd exhaust Locke's patience very soon. He followed the voice into the hot house.

"Christ almighty."

"Impressive isn't it?" There were several officers keeping themselves busy examining the crop. Locke couldn't blame them for wanting to work inside instead of out in the mist. "If you're into gardening. Which I happen to be."

Course he was. Another blot on his copy book. "I suppose so."

"They've got what they need. Liquid fertilisers, an irrigation system, intense lighting and enough heat to maintain the humidity. The living quarters are in an alcove just off this room."

"That where the coffee is?"

"I'll take you."

It was a neat little setup. Two beds, a kitchen and a TV. "Everything here as you found it?"

"Exactly." Hawley set to work with the flask. Poured out a drink and passed it over.

"Cheers." Locke took a sip. It was the real stuff, bitter and hot. Not the instant crap he'd been expecting. "Ignatius mentioned the gun. Not the murder weapon, I believe."

"Not been used for a while by the looks of things."

Locke picked up a pair of rubber gloves from the box at the side. He slipped them on and took the money belt from the middle of the table. He unzipped the first of three compartments and saw a thick wedge of cash. "Must be a lucrative business." He flicked through the notes. Reckoned it came to two grand. The other pockets carried similar amounts.

"Drug squad been informed?"

"They'll be here first thing."

"Boy, did I choose the wrong career." He wandered over to the plastic container and picked out a bag of crop. Wondered if he could sneak a few ounces for personal use. A couple of joints would definitely help with his insomnia. He looked around to check if anyone was watching. They were all too busy with their fine-tooth combs. He should be able to get a few buds without problem.

"There are plenty of crooks in our prisons who are probably thinking the same. Wishing you'd taken up with the fire service or something."

Locke smiled at that. He was pleased his reputation hadn't tarnished too badly over the years. He ripped a small hole in the bag he was holding. Dug his fingers in and sniffed hard. Thought of hippies and heavy rock gigs. "Find anything in the fridge?"

Hawley opened the door. While he was busy, Locke removed his hand and pocketed a substantial knot of leaves.

"Beer mainly."

"Shame it has to go to waste."

"It'll all be destroyed once we've finished."

"Aye."

"What shall I focus on?"

"Nothing specific. Just make sure you cover the basics. Let me know if you find anything."

"I'll do that." Hawley scratched his head. "Imagine all this going on and nobody knowing about it. It seems the cheekier you are, the more likely you are to get away with it."

"You'd better believe it." Locke had seen smaller scale operations in houses in the middle of a terrace. The neighbours never suspected a thing. "This place is certainly the biggest grow I've come across. It's got Red Fenton's fingerprints all over it."

"If it does, John, we'll find them. The team's been dusting since we arrived. They'll be doing the kitchen next."

Locke chuckled at the sergeant. "If you need me, I'll be out in my car." He took off his gloves and flicked them into the bin. "Taking notes." He wandered out into the night, passed the team putting their corpse into a body bag, and fingered the leaves inside his coat pocket.

It would be interesting to see Red Fenton again, he decided. It was always nice to mull over the good old days.

five

Brad drove through the valley, his wife already asleep and his son snoring in the back. The wipers squeaked each time they swept across the windscreen. The darkness and isolation was unnerving. The sooner they got onto the main roads, the better.

Something was wrong, Brad was sure of it. It wasn't just that his wife was now a murderer. He didn't feel right. It was as if something was missing. Like he'd left something behind. It wasn't the car keys. They were right in front of him in the ignition. He felt in the door panel. The passports were exactly where he'd left them. He eased back on the accelerator, leaned over and opened the glove compartment as quietly as he could. The light came on and revealed the purse with the key to the caravan. Next to it the gun that Molly had used at the farm.

His hand recoiled. He slammed the door shut. Opened the window enough to let clean air into the car. Oxygen was something he couldn't get enough of. It was always limited during the missions under the sea. They kept it to a minimum unless they felt the crew were in need of a boost.

He breathed deeply and let the air settle his mind. He rested his hand on his stomach pushed against the wall of solid muscle.

The realisation stunned him momentarily. He slammed on the brakes and the car skidded to a halt. Everything inside shunted forward.

"Jesus." Molly's eyes opened wide. "Did we hit something?"

Shem didn't notice a thing, just kept on whiffling in his sleep.

"The money belt. It's not here. We must have left it at the barn." He gripped the steering wheel tight. Butted it with his head. It was too soft to hurt, so he did it again twice as hard.

"You sure you didn't put it somewhere safe?"

"I'm not sure of anything just now." He opened the door. Stepped out onto the mound at the side of the road. Dropped to his knees and vomited his monk's vegetables into the spiky grass. Molly came over to comfort him. He buried his face into her midriff and shut his eyes tight. His options whirred around inside his head like helicopter blades. He'd only been AWOL for a few hours and the whole plan was turning to shit.

Maybe if he went back it would be all right. Driving up to Faslane and making up a cock-and-bull excuse might work. He could tell them Shem was sick or Molly's navigation skills had led them into the wild. They'd believe him. His record was impeccable.

If only he hadn't sent the letter to the press. That certainly complicated matters. And if he went back, there'd be another ninety-day shift looming round the corner. More time breathing in farts and BO and putting up with endless hours of practical jokes while his kid grew and his wife got itchy feet. Sod that for a lark.

"We can go back to the farm." Molly could still think clearly. "It might still be there."

Was it an option? He didn't want to see the dead bodies again or to relive the nightmare, but it made sense. They could even take a few bags of the green with them like they should have the first time round. The cushion of an extra few grand might come in useful.

"Let's do it." They rushed back into the car. Brad turned it around. He did his best to drive as quickly as he could while trying to take the blind corners and sharp bends safely enough to keep his family alive. He passed the spot where they'd stopped to make the phone call to the ambulance and knew they were almost there.

They emerged from a thick pine wood. A signpost pointed to the loch. Brad followed the directions and pulled up at the side of the road.

It was clear from a mile away they were too late. Blue lights flashed below. Police and ambulances were already on the case.

"Shit." Brad shouted through his clenched teeth. "What the hell was I thinking?" It was enough to wake Shem, who made whimpering noises in the back. Molly turned to soothe her boy while Brad did his best to keep it together.

Trying to do the right thing always seemed to backfire. Phoning the emergency services was an act of kindness and probably a wasted one at that. The Chinese guy was most likely dead. Even if he wasn't, would he really be of benefit to society if they kept him alive?

The thing with Richardson was just another example. The guy had poured out his feelings for an hour, filling the space with a pain that was too dark for either of them to handle. Brad had done his best. He listened and nodded in all the right places. He offered advice on how to survive it all. He'd even given him a bloody great hug, the kind that would have got them a ribbing for the rest of the voyage if anyone had seen. And what had it come to? One dead sailor and another who couldn't face another minute under the sea.

"It's the police. I think they're coming over." Molly sounded frightened. It might have had something to do with the fact that she was a killer who had the murder weapon not two feet from where she sat.

Brad couldn't believe he'd missed them. The police car was just ahead, its rear lights flashing.

Two uniformed constables walked over. They got to the car and split up. One took the passenger side, the other the driver's. The officer on Brad's side shone his torch onto his face. Gestured for him to open the window all the way.

The extra oxygen didn't do Brad's spirits any good. His hands shook and he wanted to throw up again.

"Is something wrong, sir?" The voice was deep and disconcerting.

"We're lost. The Sat Nav's packed in and we don't have a map. We saw the signs of life down there and stopped to have a look."

The torch circled the interior of the car. Its beam fell on Molly and then on Shem. "Sorry sir. I didn't realise you had a child in the back."

It was amazing what a difference having Shem around made. Whether it was because he was still young or that he gave off relaxing vibes, Brad was yet to work out. "We were camping. The storms flooded us out. Now we're heading back to Edinburgh." There was no way he was about to give them their real destination.

"It's lucky we ran into you. You're going the wrong way." With the light in his eyes, all Brad could see was the silhouette of a head wearing a peaked cap. "You'll need to turn around. Drive to the T-junction and take a left. Keep going through the valley for about ten miles and you'll see the signs."

"Thanks very much. It'll be good to get home."

"Drive carefully, sir."

"I will." He thought about asking what was going over at the buildings. Decided better of it. Closed the window, put the car into gear and drove.

six

"Our man still not shown up?" Commander Briggs stared out of the window like the answer wasn't important.

"I'm afraid not." Shanks sat back in his chair and pulled out a notebook from his pocket. "And it appears that Brad Heap's life isn't as boring as you might expect."

That caught Briggs's attention. Perhaps he was expecting something sexy and sordid to be thrown into the mix. "Please tell all."

"I went along to check out his accommodation. It's been emptied. There were a few toys and a couple of dresses, but that's about it."

"Dresses eh?" The commander's eyebrows rose like caterpillars squaring up to each other.

"His wife's, sir."

"Of course."

"So, we're assuming this is a planned exit."

"I don't suppose he left us with a forwarding address."

"I'm afraid not."

"Ah."

"There are some other complications to add to the picture." Shanks referred to his notes. "A Sergeant Hawley from Police Scotland was in touch first thing this morning."

The commander cleared his throat. Bad news made him nervous.

"It appears that Heap has got himself involved in a rather difficult situation."

"Bugger." Briggs stood up. Began his pacing ritual.

"That's about right, sir. At eleven fifteen last night a call was put in to the emergency services using Heap's phone. The caller was reporting a shooting incident just west of Pitlochry. The attending ambulance found one dead body and one seriously injured victim."

"Was your sergeant able to talk to the wounded chap?"

"The man hasn't regained consciousness since the surgery. It may be a while before they can ask him anything."

"I suppose it could be worse."

"Apparently it is. The men were shot outside an intensive cannabis farm. The police think that it could be part of a major organised crime syndicate."

Briggs stopped pacing. He went to the shelf behind his desk and studied his rack of pipes. "I can't see that. Heap a stoner? He simply isn't the type."

"I agree. But it seems odd that he would show up there."

The commander selected a pipe with a curved stem in the Sherlock Holmes style. "It might explain a few things, though. What if he stumbled upon this cannabis plantation? Is it not possible that some harm may have come to him? That the gangs you mention used his phone to call for help and whisked him away somewhere as a hostage? Or even put a bullet through his head and disposed of his body up in the mountains?"

It wasn't something Shanks had considered. "It wouldn't explain the empty house."

"I suppose not. Carry on making your enquiries and keep me in the loop. I'll dig around and see if I can get you working with Police Scotland." Shanks felt his face drop. "I know they don't like it when we involve ourselves, but that's because our boys are so much better than theirs."

"Sir."

"Well? What are you waiting for?"

Shanks stood. Saluted. His stomach cramped at the thought of working with civilians again.

He backed out of the room wondering how a man of Briggs's calibre managed to rise to such a dizzy rank

seven

Twelve hours in the caravan and Brad already felt like a caged animal. Molly held an ice cube to his ear while he concentrated on the early evening news. They were waiting for an update on the events of the night before. This was the third item and there hadn't been a mention.

"You ready?"

Course he was. It would only be a little prick. He'd endured much more intense pain in the name of navy humour. The staple scars that speckled his back could testify to that. "Just do it."

She kissed him on the cheek and dropped the ice into a bowl.

They were sitting on the U-shaped seat that formed the lounge of their borrowed space. It looked like a relaxing spot, but the cushions were so stiff and the angles so square it was almost impossible to get comfortable, even when you were lying down.

Molly went to the cooker and lit a gas ring. She heated the end of her needle until it glowed red and returned to the lounge. "Look up to the ceiling and think about something nice."

That wouldn't be easy. All he could focus on was money. Thirty-two pounds and change was all they had. Not a lot to run a family on. They'd be skint in a few days with no way of raising any cash other than selling the car or their wedding rings. Both options were out of the question.

Shem ran through and sat on a stool by the table. He stared as Molly positioned the point of the needle in Brad's left lobe. "Can I get an earring too, Daddy?"

"No you bloody well can't." As soon as the words were out the metal was in. He felt the heat push into his flesh and then a burst of pain exploded into his head. "What are you doing up there? Slicing the thing off?"

"Hang on a mo. It's not going through."

Shem jumped to his feet and went over for a closer inspection. "Yeuk," was all he said.

Molly knelt up on the sofa. She came down on the ear with extra weight.

The point went all the way and pricked his skull. His muscles clenched for a moment and then softened again. "Easy tiger. There's no oil in here you know."

She kissed him on the mouth and ruffled Shem's hair. "Now all you need to do is to choose an earring to match your outfit."

The newsreader mentioned the cannabis farm.

"Quiet now." Brad turned up the volume. "Let's see what's going on in the real world."

It was the same piece that they ran at lunch time. Police have uncovered another major source of drugs production in Scotland. They were sure this discovery would lead to the closing down of similar operations throughout the country. "Cut off the dragon's head," the public relations officer told a reporter, "and the body soon comes crashing to the ground." So far there was no mention of Molly or Brad as suspects. The police were going be continuing their enquiries.

"There'll probably be more on the local news." She chewed at her fingernails for a moment, then caught herself and snatched her hand back. It wasn't a good sign. Her nails were her pets, always well-looked after and lavished with attention. Just keeping her in varnish for a week would blow their entire savings.

Brad felt his heart empty. He opened his arms and invited his family in for a hug. Molly came in from the left, Shem from the right. He grabbed hold and allowed their love to fill him up again.

"Right then, who's up for a game of Monopoly?"

Molly and Shem threw their hands into the air and cheered.

Shem ran off to get the board and Molly wiped the table down. Brad poked a silver stud through his piercing and slotted the butterfly clip onto the back. He realised just how much he needed his family with him. He also knew that the only thing that would really settle his nerves was a drink.

*

The Smugglers Inn was an old-time pub. Wooden benches. Real ale on tap. A few bottles of the hard stuff on the shelves, but nothing fancy. The light was low and the walls were still yellow from the days of indoor smoking. There was a tiny snug off behind the bar for those wanting to avoid the limelight. The barman looked as ancient as the building. He didn't move much, but his eyes shifted warily around the room as if he was uncomfortable having a stranger on the scene. There was no music which suited Brad just fine.

He sat at a table by the door, nursing a pint and a shot of whisky. The drinks had cost him a fair chunk of their funds, but it couldn't be helped. He might even go wild and pick up a bottle of cheap wine from the store later on. Share it with Molly and ease his guilt. See if they couldn't find a silver lining, even if it would only last for one night.

His ear hurt. Not that he would admit it to anyone. It burned and throbbed. The only way to relieve the pain was to twist his new stud around in the hole.

It was quiet tonight. Probably always was on a Monday. Every so often there were a few guffaws from out the back. In the main bar was a couple who sat in virtual silence in the corner. They leant in towards each other when they spoke as if their secrets were too important to be overheard. The woman looked too young to be drinking, the lad too worldly-wise to be doing anything else.

Watching them put Brad on edge. Every time the girl touched the man he pulled back. The body language was stiff and aggressive and his stare seemed designed to intimidate his lover rather than woo her. No doubt it was building to something. Brad hoped he could enjoy his drinks and get out of there before anything kicked off.

He picked up his whisky and swirled it around the glass, sniffing up the fumes as they filled the air. They smelled of earth. He took a sip. The fiery malt gave him a sting as it went down. It was exactly the feeling he was after. He dipped his fingers into his drink and dabbed them onto his piercing. Cleaning it would help it to heal.

The Shallows

"No!" The shout came from the man in the corner. He stood and bared his teeth at the girl. He stepped out from his seat and grabbed his girlfriend by the shoulders. He pulled her down and her head bashed the table. Their glasses went flying. A helpless squeal escaped her mouth and the man pushed on her neck, so hard that the veins in his solid forearms bulged. He bent low. Got right up to the girl's face and growled something inaudible.

Brad reacted without thinking. He leapt from his seat and jogged over. The thug provided an easy target. With one hand Brad grabbed the knot in the man's hair. With the other Brad turned the guy's arm behind his back so that his wrist was right between the shoulder blades. Something cracked inside, but Brad didn't care. He pulled him away and thumped his head into the wall once, twice, three times. Brad felt the knees give way and let the body slump onto the bench. To keep safe, he extended the thug's arm, gave it a half-turn and held it securely by the palm. Were he to use his elbow to bang down on the twisted limb, the bones would snap. He wasn't bothered whether he had to take it that far or not.

The lad bucked a couple of times. Saliva flew from his mouth as he made the effort. He was strong and solid, but there was nothing he could do.

"Enough." The voice came from the bar. It was firm and persuasive. Brad looked up to check what was going on, careful to maintain his grip and his advantage.

The girl jumped up and ran to the man who had entered. She held onto the chest of a giant with faded ginger hair. "Dad," she sobbed. "Gary's been seeing someone else. And he attacked me when I challenged him about it."

The father took the girl's chin between a finger and thumb and lifted her face upwards. He shifted it from side to side and assessed the damage. His cheeks reddened and his nostrils flared.

"And you?" He stared at Brad now. "What have you got to do with all this?"

Brad altered his hold and shunted his knee into the spine of the man he was pinning down. "I'm the innocent bystander. I came in to have a quick drink and this loser decided to ruin the atmosphere."

The big guy smiled. "I guess I should thank you for saving my little girl." And his smile vanished. "You can let him go. He won't do anything rash now I'm here, will you Gary?"

Gary nodded his head as far as he could manage, pressed down as it was into the table and a puddle of booze.

"I'm loosening my grip. Can you feel that?" It was a rule Brad stuck with. Always explain your actions. Keep the upper hand and make sure there are no false moves. Control the situation to the last. "When I let go, I want you to step away from me and sit down on the chair. You as much as turn my way and I'm putting you down." He lessened the pressure on the wrist and removed his knee.

Gary stood. His legs wobbled when they took his weight. He rubbed his jaw and sat just as he'd been told.

"Good boy."

"Listen Red." Gary's voice was thin and weak. "I'm sorry about what I done. Honest to God."

Brad wanted to melt away. He walked back over to his table and downed the remains of his whisky.

"Sorry's just a word Gary. When you've heard it as many times as I have, it means nothing. It's actions that make the difference. By the looks of things, what you've been up to isn't very nice." Red stroked his daughter's hair. "You go home, pet. Tell your mam all about it. I'll give Gary a bit of advice and we'll see if we can't sort it this evening." He gave her a gentle push towards the exit.

"You won't hurt him, will you Dad?"

"Course not."

She seemed satisfied by that, picked up her bag and her jacket and muttered something to Gary as she left the pub.

It was Gary who spoke first once the door closed. "I've never let you down, Red. You know I haven't."

"That's true. You've worked hard for me, I'll be sorry to see you go."

"Go? You can't get rid of me. Especially now Junior's dead. Who'll do the work on the next trip?"

"There's always someone needs a job in these parts, Gary. Long as they can keep their mouth shut and know their way around a boat, I'll give them a chance."

The flesh around Gary's eyes was turning puffy. It looked like he was about to cry. "What happened with Trish, that was nothing. It was just the beer goggles, that's all."

"You ever heard the advice about not shitting on your own doorstep?"

Gary nodded again. He sat up straight, rocking as if suddenly in desperate need of the toilet.

"Well it's time you found yourself another doorstep."

"What do you mean?"

"I mean make yourself scarce. Get out of town. I see your face around here again and I won't be responsible for what happens."

"You told Kylie you wouldn't hurt me."

"Don't be daft. I wouldn't dirty my knuckles. I'll find someone else to do it for me. Someone much bigger and meaner than I am."

Gary thought about it. "So I'm sacked?"

"Yep."

"And I have to leave Eyemouth?"

"Soon as."

"And that'll be us square?"

"It will."

"Then I'll do it." Gary stood up. He adjusted the knot of hair on the top of his head and backed slowly over to the door. He pulled it open and slipped out. The sound of his footsteps running up the street made it clear he was in a hurry.

"Now young fellow." Red turned to Brad. "I'd like to have a quiet word in my office back here if you don't mind." He looked over to the barman who had miraculously reappeared from nowhere. "Get this gentleman whatever he had before. "And another for me and Sid while you're at it."

He sauntered into the snug, rolling up his sleeves and laughing hard. Brad picked up his beer and followed. If he could pick up a few quid for his knight-in-shining-armour routine, it might not end up being such a bad night after all.

*

The snug was narrow and even darker than the main bar. The cushions on the benches made it look cosy. There were only two tables. The first was occupied by a frail looking pensioner with a half of stout in front of him and a grey whippet at his feet. The dog had beautiful sad eyes and lay with its long snout on its paws.

"Here's the new kid on the block, Sid."

"Hiya." Sid raised his cap a couple of millimetres and let it drop back again. "Told you to watch out for that Gary. I knew he was rotten."

"Aye, well. That's enough about him. Let's find out a little more about our hero shall we? I don't think I've seen you around here before."

The barman delivered the drinks. A whisky and a pint for Brad, a bottle of brown ale for Red and another stout for Sid.

"Cheers. No, I'm not from these parts."

"Where did you learn to handle yourself like that?"

Brad took a long sip of his beer. The alcohol had taken the edge from his woes and the adrenaline from the action had him ready for anything the world could throw him. "Navy." There didn't seem to be much point lying. Besides, straying too far from the truth was the most likely way for him to become undone.

"Knew it." Red poured his ale into the glass and belched. Filled the room with the smell of pork scratchings. "I was a Para. Till the asthma got me the boot. You still in?"

"Looking for work."

Sid and Red exchanged glances.

"Preferably cash in hand." Until Brad could raise the money to sort out a set of false identification, any jobs he took on had to be on an off-the-books basis.

The Shallows

"It might just be that I have something for you. It'll mean a night away on the boat, mind. And whatever happens while we're at sea stays there. You understand?"

It sounded dodgy as hell. A clear-headed Brad wouldn't have touched it. A desperate one trying to forge a new life for his family with a fund of twenty-five quid to set things up was ready to jump at the chance. Besides, what had doing the right thing ever got him other than into a whole pile of crap? "Give me a time and a place and I'll be there."

"Show up at the harbour on Wednesday around tea time. Check out the fishing boat *Sriga*. If I'm not there, tell them Red sent you."

"I'll be there."

"What name shall I give the skip?"

He considered creating something on the spot. Decided against. "Brad."

"I'll drink to your health. Here's to the start of a beautiful friendship." He lifted his glass. The others did the same.

Brad asked for a pen.

The barman passed over a cheap bookies biro. On his hand, Brad wrote Wednesday. Six o'clock. *Sriga*. The name of the boat triggered a memory. About ship's names ending in *A* being unlucky. He tried to recall who'd told him that. Shrugged off the superstition. He'd had enough bad luck in the past weeks to last him a lifetime.

eight

John Locke drove past a playground on the outskirts of town. A gang of kids enjoying the tail-end of their summer holidays played football on the grass. On the side-lines, a group of lads with bare chests wrestled as if they meant business. The girls on the swings smoked and fiddled with their phones.

He turned right and passed a high school that hadn't been there on his last visit. It was expensive-looking and was dominated by a curved entrance hall. If it was as impressive on the inside as it was at first viewing, the kids he'd just seen on the rec might have hope of a future.

On the roundabout, a freshly painted boat filled with soil and plants told him *WELCOME TO EYEMOUTH*. A fishing net and a couple of lobster pots thrown on the grass added to the scene. You had to admire a place taking pride in itself like this. For putting a positive slant on difficult times. It wasn't easy standing up when you were on your knees, Locke understood that well.

The lampposts on either side of the road carried placards that flapped in the breeze. They carried pictures of the Herring Queens going back over the years. How things had changed. The women from the fifties, the decade in which Locke was born, looked as though they modelled themselves on Elizabeth Rex.

1959, overweight and sporting thick NHS glasses, was a Rex of a different kind altogether. Locke wondered what she was doing now. Whether she'd even be alive. The thought depressed him and he stopped paying attention. He took a cigarette from the box on the passenger seat and lit up. The smoke cleared his head, and he drove on through and parked up outside the Co-op just off the promenade.

For old-times' sake, he wandered over to the penny arcade with the huge plastic ice cream out front. The room stretched out before of him and the noises came from everywhere. When Locke was growing up, a place like this would have been packed out in August. Today he was the only customer.

The Shallows

Locke strolled past the 2p machines checking for any that seemed ready to spill. His gaze scanned the floor as he went, a habit from his childhood. He found nothing. At the racing machine he stopped and searched his pockets. Among a pile of change he found the coin he needed to place a bet. The horses returned to the start. Locke checked the odds and dropped his money into the slot. Backed the outsider, just like always. The favourite won. A small fanfare piped it home. Locke tapped the glass top to acknowledge his failure and walked back out into the salty air.

The promenade was busy with dog-walkers, old-folk and the unemployed. They gazed out at the sea as if it had broken a promise. Locke kept his eyes forward. Didn't want his life dissolving into the waves. He strode out until he got to the harbour and stopped to admire the view.

It was rare to see a working port with fishing boats and a decent set-up. This was still the real deal. From the dry dock came the sounds of hammers banging steel. On the rocks a family of seals basked in the sunshine. Fishermen readied their craft for the next trip out. Gulls circled overhead, the nearest thing to vultures Scotland could provide. Their cries were loud and insistent and could go through your head like a drill if you didn't block them out. Looking down on the scene was the ever so grand Gunsgreen House, home to many a smuggler in its day. There were secret tea chutes behind the wall and the position made it perfect for the easy transfer of tobacco and brandy from ship to shore. To some, the building represented finer times for the town. To Locke, it merely reminded him that the inhabitants had deception running through their veins where there should have been blood. Their iniquities had been around for generations and would be there for a good while yet as long as folk like Red Fenton stuck around.

Locke smiled to himself and walked over towards the market. He stopped at the small fishmonger's, noted the deal on breaded haddock and went in.

The man behind the counter didn't bother to say hello. He just stood there in his waterproof apron and silly hat and glowered. Tucked into his string belt were sharp-looking knives that looked capable of gutting anything that came their way. The fish were arranged as if they were exhibits in a gallery. They were grouped by colour and organised by size. Shells and seaweed decorated the spaces between. In the centre, a large cod head emerged from the ice like a monster from the deep. With all those eyes staring up at him, Locke felt like he was under surveillance.

"Still here Archie? I thought you'd have retired years ago."

Archie blew an answer through his nose, sounding like an angry bull that had glimpsed the toreador. Pointed to the doorway at the back with his thumb.

"May I go through?"

The fishmonger pulled a phone from his back pocket. Dialled a number and waited. "There's someone here to see you. One of her Majesty's finest. That old bollocks with the walrus moustache and the toupee. Yeah, that one." He looked over at Locke. "The boss wants to know if it's business or pleasure."

"Strictly business."

"He says it's business." A pause. "I'll tell him." He pressed a button and put the moblie back into his jeans. "Twenty minutes tops."

"That's all I need." Locke walked over to the doorway and turned around. "The hair's real, I'll have you know." He brushed the parting into place. "Be a good man and bag up a nice monkfish and your four nicest scallops while I'm gone. I'll pick them up on the way out." He took the steps two at a time. His heart was beating fast when he got to the top.

He smelled Red before he saw him. It was a unique scent. A mongrel mix that lay somewhere between salty damp dog and yeasty Newcastle Brown.

Locke ducked his head and entered the lair.

The Shallows

Red was sitting at the far end of a long table behind a set of tins of modeller's paint and a large wooden sailing ship. His hair had lost something of its brightness over the years, yet he was still a strapping bloke. In his hands, a paintbrush and mug. He didn't take his eyes from the vessel as Locke approached.

"It's been a while." Red put down his tea and added colour to the tallest mast.

"Not long enough." He pulled out a chair. "May I?"

"Help yourself."

"You've been busy." The room was packed with model boats and ships. They occupied all the available shelves and counters.

"A man needs a hobby otherwise he'll drown in all the spare time."

"I'll have to remember to get one."

"You do that."

"I don't see any of your heavies around." Last time he'd been here, the muscle was everywhere.

"That's because I don't need them anymore. I retired." He dipped his brush into a jar of white spirit and wiped it clean. "I still hang on to Archie, though. He's usually enough to put off anyone who bears a grudge."

"I can't believe you've given it all up. A man like you gets the opposite of sea-sickness when he's on land for too long."

"I spend plenty of time on the water. Recreational trips for sightseers and the like"

Locke reached into his jacket pocket. He took out an envelope, removed a set of photographs and laid them out on the table. He pushed the snap of Sammy Davis over and waited for a reaction.

"Junior." Red picked it up and shook his head. "He's not looking so well. You should have taken it from his good side."

"I believe he works for you."

"Used to. Until I gave it up."

"When was the last time you saw him?"

"Three years or more. He went walkabout. Had big plans and dreams. A place like this wasn't going to satisfy him. Eyes bigger than his belly. He wasn't destined for happiness."

"Ever hear from him?"

"Not so much as a Christmas card."

"I always got the impression you two were tight."

"We were never generous, if that's what you mean."

Very funny. Locke slid over the picture of the Chinese man. "Know this one?"

"Looks like the guys in the takeaway down the street."

"And I don't suppose you know anything about this either." This time, the pictures showed off the cannabis farm.

"Where's this? The Amazon?"

"A bit closer to home."

"That new garden centre in Berwick?"

"Wrong again. It's the plantation where Junior was killed."

"He'd moved out to the tropics? I hadn't marked him down as the adventurous sort."

"Didn't get past Inverness, I'm afraid."

"Not to worry. At least he died on his own ground." He adjusted the mast on the model ship. Took out a magnifying glass and studied it.

Red was playing stonewall, just as Locke expected. If all he'd wanted was the truth, he wouldn't have bothered coming all this way. Putting on a little pressure and forcing him into some movement, that was what this was about. You can't always unblock a toilet by using the flush alone. At least that's what his mentor had taught him back in the day. "Where were you on Sunday evening?"

"Which Sunday are we talking about?"

The slippery sod. "The one just gone."

"Time?"

"Eleven."

"That's easy. I was at the Smugglers. I'm usually there around then."

"Anyone vouch for that?" Locke took out his notebook. He could at least spend a few minutes checking the alibi.

The Shallows

"Let me think." He selected a screwdriver and forced the lid off one of the small tins.

The oily smell evoked Locke's childhood. The nostalgia made him glow for a moment as he pictured his Airfix model of a spitfire. The pleasure faded to nought when he recalled his brother smashing it after an argument.

Red dipped his brush into the paint. He set to work on the crow's nest and turned it into a darker shade of brown. "Bob the barman. That goes without saying. And Sid. You remember him, I'm sure."

Locke made a note of the names. "Sid's still alive?"

"It's not always easy to tell."

"Never was." Sid lived in the shadows. Had fingers reaching into pies across The Borders and down into Northumberland once-upon-a-time. Did a few stretches in prison for minor offences, but they couldn't pin any of the big stuff on him. "He still working?"

"Too sensible. Nearest he gets to crime these days is when he's watching TV."

"Good to know." Locke closed his pad and stood up. "That's me done. Finished with a good few minutes to spare."

"Very kind of you to make it short. Next time you think about making a visit, save yourself the bother and stay home."

"Hear anything about Junior, I'd appreciate a call." He didn't bother to take a card from his wallet. "And keep up the work on your toys." He pointed at some of the models around the room. "By the looks of things, you're definitely improving."

The brush slipped from between Red's fingers. It dropped onto the boat's deck and left a tiny splodge of paint. He stamped the floor and the table shook. "You know the way out."

The glower in Red's eyes put an exclamation mark at the end of his sentence. The interview was over. It was time for Locke to pick up his fish and leave.

*

There was no point going home. All that waited for him there was a pair of worn slippers and a bottle.

He didn't fancy returning to the station either. The chances were that Hawley or Shanks would be there poring through the paperwork and searching their computers hoping to find a thread to get hold of. The less he had to do with that officious pair, the better.

Instead, Locke went to Mackie's and splashed out on an ice cream in a waffle cone. His doctor wouldn't be happy about the calories or the sugar content, but the chunks of soft chocolate brownie were definitely helping with the sense of well-being.

He sat on a bench at the head of the harbour and settled himself down. There wasn't a great deal of mystery to police work. You let the teams in the labs collect the evidence and point the way. Allowed your instincts to drag you where they would and made sure you put in the hours until everything fell into place. A lot of it was about watching and waiting, two things Locke was expert in.

It was a beautiful evening. The breeze was light and the sun warmed his skin. He wiped his fingers on a paper serviette and put on a pair of sunglasses. He took out a cigarette and lifted it to his lips. As he lit it and sucked in the first smoke, Red and Archie came out of the shop. Archie locked the door and pulled the shutters down over the window.

With their bulk emphasised by their leather jackets, the pair looked like bouncers from a seedy nightclub. They set off walking as if leaving the town. At the pontoon bridge, they crossed the water and turned back on themselves. They passed the biggest trawlers and then stopped.

Archie swung himself onto the steps and climbed down. Red followed. They boarded a nice looking craft that had to be at least twenty metres long. It was sunshine yellow along the hull. The wheelhouse, the bow and the masts were white. Locke thought he recognised it from Red's room full of models. It carried the winches, nets and boxes of a working vessel. Red and Archie disappeared into the cabin.

The Shallows

      Locke finished his cigarette and wandered over to the edge. He admired the lines of the craft below and took out his pad. He wrote down the name *Sriga* and the numbers painted on the side, underlined it all twice and decided to call it a night.

nine

The food bank was in an old stone building, tucked out of the way down a side-street close to the centre of town. Molly stood and stared at it, trying to convince herself to go in. Her palms were sweating. She felt vulnerable, as if she were about to be exposed to the world. Shem was beside her eating his apple and watching roofers working a few houses further down.

A huge lady pushing a corroded shopping trolley waddled by on the opposite pavement. Her legs were thick as an elephant's and her tight leggings did nothing for her. She seriously needed fashion advice. A baggy dress or a loose fitting top that came down far enough to cover her backside could make all the difference. Maybe some bright colours in the fabric to distract the eye. She parked the trolley outside the door and took a suck on an inhaler.

"The last thing that woman needs is anything else to eat." Molly had her down as a scrounger. A no-good layabout whose only exercise was pressing the button on the TV remote.

"It's probably not her fault, Mum. It might just be the way she is. That's what my teacher said." Shem finished his fruit and dropped the core into the bin.

Molly hugged her son. "I'm sorry. Miss Stones was right. I don't suppose anyone would choose to be as fat as that. Are you ready?"

Shem nodded. The pair crossed the road and followed the big lady through the door.

The room went back a long way. Bed-sheets hanging on a line acted as a divider between the front of house and the storage area. Through the gap, Molly saw shelves packed with goods and a couple of old folk sorting things out on pasting tables.

"All right Nancy? How are you keeping?" A gentleman in a V-necked sweater and pink tie came from around the makeshift counter. He went over to the chair in the corner and picked up the ginger cat that slept there.

"Can't complain." Nancy took a seat. A gasp escaped from the cushion as her frame landed. "The bairn's much better now. It was just arthritis brought on by a virus."

"Glad to hear it." The man opened the door. Placed the cat on the pavement, gave it a gentle push and came back in. "Is that your trolley?"

Nancy nodded.

"I'll just get the stuff." He slid a brick over to the door to keep it open and turned to the store room. "We've got a rush on Maureen."

Maureen entered the room. So did the smell of stale sweat. Her hair was cropped short and her skin tough. If you took the breasts away she would have looked like a bloke. "Yes. What can we do you for?"

"My son and I, we're hungry. We want to get some food, please."

"Oh aye?" Maureen pushed up her sleeves and folded her arms across her chest. "Who sent you?" Her tone was aggressive and cold.

"Nobody. We came down all by ourselves."

"So you haven't gone through the referral process?"

"Process?"

"The usual channels. Social work. Church. Personal recommendation."

"No. None of those."

The man in the V-neck stepped out from the back with a huge cardboard box. It looked like he was struggling. Maureen would have managed much better. He walked backwards through the doorway and out onto the street.

"Then I'm afraid we can't offer you assistance." Maureen sucked at her teeth and pursed her lips.

Molly was devastated. The only thing worse than asking for a hand-out was being turned down for one. Tears warmed her eyes and her throat tightened. "But you help the hungry." Her voice sounded like a radio with poor reception. "That's what you do."

"Not if they don't come with a referral we don't. Otherwise we just end up with a bunch of scroungers and imposters trying to live on the cheap when they can afford to manage perfectly well." The woman's expression didn't change as she spoke. If she were a coffee, she'd be a flat white. She picked up a sheet of paper from a box-file and handed it over. "Here's all the information you need. As soon as you've gone through the process, we'll put you on our books and you'll be entitled to regular support."

Shem looked up at Molly. He reached out and took her hand. His small fingers squeezed hard.

The man returned, all smiles and good cheer. "I'll just get the other one Nancy. I won't be a sec." His words made a happy tune.

"That's grand Alf. I owe you."

"You don't owe me a thing. It's Our Lord you need to thank. Come along to church on Sunday to pay your respects. That's all the reward I seek."

"You're too kind."

Shem turned to Maureen. "Do you people all believe in God?" There was nothing challenging in his tone.

"Why, of course."

"And you live by the teachings of Jesus?"

"Nobody's perfect, but we do our best."

"If my mum went to him and asked for some food, don't you think he'd give it?"

"Not without the paperwork he wouldn't."

"You're wrong." Shem pushed his glasses back on his nose and nodded. "He'd do a miracle. I know he would. He'd magic something to eat from nothing and hand to us. That's what he did. Gave to the people who needed it and who had clean hearts."

Molly's insides shook. She was proud of her son for his courage and his support, yet knew that ever since she killed those men her heart was darker than that of a hardened smoker. She brushed away the tears that ran down her face.

Maureen remained silent. Her shoulders dropped a little and her nose wrinkled up.

Alf walked out with the second box. "This one's even got chocolate. I saved it for you especially." He winked at Nancy and went outside.

Nancy cleared her throat. "Can't you bend things a little? Just this once?"

"You know the way it works. God knows you've been taking from us for long enough to understand. The rules are the rules and I'm not going to break them for anything." She wiped something invisible from the counter with her fingers. "Like I said, come back when you've done what it tells you on that letter and we'll give you plenty."

This time Molly's emotions burst. The sobs poured from her and she hid her face with her hands.

"What's the matter, Honey?" Nancy forced herself up from the chair. "Can't you read the forms?"

"She can read really well." Shem stepped in between the two women and stood at his full height, shoulders squared like his father did when he wanted to make a point.

"I didn't mean to offend your mother." Her smile was warm and kind. "I was just trying to help." Nancy pulled a tissue from under the sleeve of her T-shirt and passed it over.

Molly sniffed and took it. "Thanks." She blew her nose and wiped her eyes and offered to pass it back.

"You can keep it. I may be hard up, but I can spare a tissue every now and then."

"Of course." Even though Molly felt empty, she laughed. Shem joined in and the atmosphere lightened. "I'll do these forms and hand them in." Living under the radar meant she couldn't. Getting supplies from the food bank was out of the question. She needed a plan B. The few pounds she had would have to keep them going until she thought of one.

The large lady leaned across. "Take no notice of Maureen. She looks fierce, but she's a total dragon when you get to know her."

Maureen tutted and walked off into the storeroom. "I'll remember that."

Alf popped his head in. "All locked and loaded."

"That'll be me then," Nancy said to Molly and Shem. "It's worst the first time. After that, your pride settles down and pretends not to look. Come with me a sec. I've got a little something for you." She turned away and shuffled through the exit, giving Alf a kiss on the cheek as she went past. His face took on the colour of his tie. "See you at the Legion at the weekend?"

"Wouldn't miss it." He kept hold of the door while Molly and Shem left. "Thanks for coming along. We'll see you again, too."

Molly couldn't find any words. She nodded as she walked out to the pavement and watched Alf disappear back into the shop.

Nancy reached into one of the boxes in her trolley. She pulled out a yellow lollipop and held it out for Shem. "Told you I had a little something for you."

Shem looked at the lolly and shook his head.

"No need to be shy. Alf always puts in a couple for my girls. I've got more, honest."

It was all the encouragement he needed. "Thank you very much."

"Not a problem." The way Nancy spoke made Molly warm on the inside. "Now it's your mum's turn."

This time, Nancy removed the smaller box from her trolley and held it out.

"I couldn't." Molly didn't want to take the food from this kind woman's table. "It's for your children."

"They could do with losing a few inches around their waistline. Take after their mother in that respect."

Molly remembered her first impressions of Nancy and suddenly felt terribly ashamed. "I really couldn't."

"Course you can." She turned and clicked the brake from trolley. "We're all in this together. The sooner we all realise that, the better the world will be." Without waiting for any more protests, Nancy set off for home. "Enjoy."

The Shallows

"I will." Molly wanted to run after the woman and give her an enormous hug. Instead, she looked at her new supplies. Clocked the bars of chocolate, the porridge oats, the filled pasta and the jars of tomato sauce. She saw the joy on Shem's face, the lollipop stick poking out from his mouth and the look of sugary love in his eyes. "Bless you," she whispered to whatever forces had brought about this act of kindness

ten

It didn't take a genius to realise that Brad Heap and his family had nothing to do with the drugs business. Just looking at the pattern of the fingerprints in the building told Locke that. Throw in the fact that they reported the shooting and they seemed to be in the clear.

Locke did his best to picture the scene. The Scottish west coast tries to ruin another holiday by chucking it down for days on end. The Heaps get sick and tired of being wet. Maybe their tent leaks – they always do in the end – and they go in search of shelter. Brad Heap being Absent Without Leave rules out a hotel stay. They find the nearest derelict building. Stumble into a tropical rainforest and think their luck's in. Junior and Wong arrive and get twitchy. Heap picks up one of the gangsters' own guns and takes them out. Killing was what the Navy were trained for, so pulling the trigger was probably an easy thing for him to do.

The Heaps needed to be found, but Locke would be happier if they focussed on the real criminals. Red Fenton and his crew.

He licked the sticky strip on the paper he'd just rolled and finished off constructing the perfect spliff. He put the cone to his lips and lit the knot at the end. The smoke kicked him in the back of the throat and burned away at his lungs. He fought hard to keep it inside, waited for the buzz in his head and exhaled.

It was good shit that Junior was growing. He lifted the joint in salute to the dead man and turned to his computer screen.

He studied the images from the Eyemouth harbour webcam. There wasn't much happening. He checked the list of the comings and goings of boats throughout the day. The geeks who put this together were doing a solid job. There were lists of names, numbers, nationalities, type of craft and times of arrival. Locke scanned through the information. Saw nothing of interest. Took another pull on his joint and minimised the page.

The Shallows

He logged in at Forever Young, the dating site he favoured.

There were two nudges awaiting him.

The first came from Sylvia, who liked books and films and wanted companionship on her cinema visits. She could have loved bondage and lap-dancing and Locke wouldn't have gone for her. Her makeup was trowelled on and her hair dyed so black that the scalp beneath gleamed in the camera flash. Mutton dressed as lamb and not doing a very good job of it. Give her a couple of years, she'd be bald and her broken nose would still point towards her left ear.

He pressed delete and went to the second message.

Doreen. Green eyes and greying hair kept in place with an Alice band. She fell into the fifty to sixty age bracket. Her interests were wine and food and her personal statement just read '*I'm tired of being alone*'. Locke burst out laughing at that. It was either funny or the dope had a hold of him already. "What the hell."

His fingers typed quickly.

"Hi Doreen. I know where you're coming from. DM me and let's see where we get to, eh? John." He pressed send before he changed his mind, supped from his mug of tea and picked up his notebook.

He turned to the page he'd filled out at the harbour master's. Remembered what he should be doing and switched back to the webcam.

Bingo.

Sriga was emerging from the dock and heading towards the exit.

He was a genius. A study of the tide-times and knowledge of the boat's sailing patterns had led to this success. Now he could put his plan into operation. It was a simple idea. Pay attention to when the boat went out and he'd be able to meet her when she came back. That way he could find out exactly what Red's cargo was and work out from there what he was going to do about it.

Nailing the old bastard would be the perfect end to Locke's career. One loose end fewer to keep him awake at night when he retired.

To celebrate his success he relit up his smoke and took another toke. In his notebook he made a note of the time and worked out when he'd have to leave the next morning. Four o'clock seemed about right. No rest for the very wicked, he thought.

His mouth was dry. God this stuff was good. The munchies were on their way. He went to the kitchen to whip something up. A Spanish tortilla and some battered squid would do the job. Perhaps a handful of chocolate Hobnobs for dessert.

eleven

There were seven crew aboard *Sriga*. They assembled at six and left port at eight in the evening. Four hours later, Brad still had little idea of what anyone expected of him.

Red stayed up in the wheelhouse with the skipper, an old salt called Docherty. They were the only men on the ship who were doing any actual work.

Brad was down below reading his book under the pathetic amount of light provided by his lamp. The others were all sleeping, a couple in the bunks, the rest wrapped in blankets on the floor. They were cut from the same cloth. Hard men who didn't have much to say.

It was odd being on the surface rather than under it. The whole experience felt different. The motion of the waves calmed him and there was noise from outside even though there was nothing out there but water and wind. He looked through the porthole. The moon, the stars and the green glow of the starboard lamp took the edge from the darkness. Life on top was so much better than the one down in the depths.

The room they occupied was less well looked after than the rest of the boat. The wood was cheap veneer and lots of it had peeled away to show the boards beneath. There was a table where they'd gathered earlier to play cards, alongside which was a bench that doubled up as storage. The cushion on top had split in several places and the foam was held in with tape. A small TV with a slot for DVDs stood on a stand in the corner. It was out of action on account of the batteries in the remote being flat.

An electric buzz interrupted the peace as the speaker above the table crackled into life. The static turned into words. "Right you lazy buggers." The skipper. "There's our connection. You know what to do." There was movement in the blankets. Stretching and moaning.

First out of bed was a lanky young lad with fluff for a beard. He went over to the bench. Lifted the cushion, opened the storage hatch and leaned in. Pulled out an Uzi sub-machine gun and threw the strap over his shoulder.

"This better go smoothly." A man in a Rangers top walked over and stopped. "I've got tickets for the first home game." Bumfluff passed him a weapon and did the same for all the others.

Brad closed his book. Tried not to show any signs of anxiety. He wondered why he'd not been given anything. Didn't want to be empty handed if the shit hit the fan. "What about me?"

The guy in the football strip came over. "Sorry pal. You're the newbie. You'll get Gary's job. Go see Red and he'll tell you what to do. Better be quick, mind. You're on first."

Christ. Being first was exactly the worst place for him to be right now. Brad went to the back of the room. He zipped up his immersion suit, grabbed a life-jacket and strapped it on. The men behind him laughed. Brad didn't care. He knew what the sea could do and understood that those who didn't respect her were playing a risky game. He walked up the ladder up onto the deck. First thing he saw was the ship just off the starboard bow, a beast of a vessel looming down.

He opened the door.

The wheelhouse was in good shape. Had more screens to look at than a bookmaker's.

Red stared right at him, hard enough to knock a smaller man down. "Suits you Brad. Must be your colour." Not funny. "What I need from you is to place the fenders between the boats then secure the walkway when it's lowered. After we're done, it's the same, only backwards." He lifted a handgun from a drawer and slipped it into the pocket of his oilskin. "Understand?"

Brad nodded. It sounded perfectly straightforward.

The skipper didn't take his eyes off the ship outside. He was a hulk of a man with a tough complexion whose sailing cap seemed to be glued onto his head at an odd angle. He made tiny turns of the wheel. Shifted the throttle into reverse and then back to idle. "Fuckers."

Who he was talking to, Brad had no idea. He left them to their manoeuvres and returned to the deck to do his job.

The Shallows

The hull of the other vessel came close and a bright beam shone into Brad's eyes. He blinked the shock away and shaded the view with his arm.

Two sailors leaned over the side above him. They threw down buffers and shouted out in a language Brad couldn't figure. A rope fell at his feet. Brad picked it up and wrapped it around the cleat. He did the same with the next and waited.

A gangway appeared. It was lowered towards him and landed with a thump on the deck. The metal was light and flimsy. It could easily have been knocked together in someone's back yard from an old greenhouse frame.

There was no obvious way to secure it. He scanned his surroundings hoping to spot something to use. All he could find was more rope. He took it, wrapped it through the bars and tied it around one of the heavy winches.

Before he could do any more he was brushed aside. Two men from the bunks were clearly impatient to get back to bed as soon as they could. They strode up the platform onto the other ship as if they were on a mission.

More shouts. Lots of waving arms.

Someone stepped on the ramp. He walked down, holding tight to the rails as he moved. Even with the ships tethered tightly together, it wobbled as he came. He was followed immediately by another body, then another. A string of faces in a line were heading straight for Brad.

The first person made it across. Had the handsome caramel shade of a North African. He offered his hand and Brad took it without thinking. The man's grin was enormous. His teeth shone white. He babbled on in happy tones and practically shook Brad's arm from its socket.

Someone grabbed the man's shoulder. Pulled him away. A pointing gun acted as a signpost telling the newcomer where to go.

Red waited across the way. Ushered the new passenger to the ladders and watched him descend.

The next to arrive on board was a boy. Couldn't have been much older than Shem. The lad kissed Brad's hand and followed the first.

It went on for a while. Brad counted to thirty then gave up.

When there were no more migrants left to board, Red walked into the cabin. He returned carrying a case. He went over to the walkway, climbed to the top and disappeared.

Over at the hold, Bumfluff and the Rangers fan slid the roof closed and set about covering it with a tarp. It didn't take them long. By the time they finished, Red had come back down onto *Sriga* with a different bag. "Let's get a wriggle on. Untie us and get us on home."

Brad did what he was told and watched the other ship pull away until it disappeared into the darkness. He thought about what had just taken place. Considered the fate of the cargo he was carrying. The migrants below clearly wanted to be there. It wasn't like Red was trafficking young girls for sex or anything. Brad recalled the pictures he'd seen of the attempts of the dispossessed crossing the Mediterranean in boats, crammed to the gunnels until they were almost sinking. How desperate they must have been to even try. They were clearly risking their lives and spending their entire wealth on trying to escape from something. Whatever it was, it was terrible and he wasn't going to feel bad about working under the radar to save a few souls. It was just another example of God working in mysterious ways.

He returned to the galley, slipped off his life-jacket and shoved it back in its cupboard.

The other four men gathered at the table, cans of ale in their hands. They hadn't left room for Brad and made no effort to welcome him in.

He needed a way to crack the barriers. Something to give him credibility. To elevate him above the rank of cabin boy and to let them know he might be sticking around for a while. Establish that he was an outsider, just like them. "That went well."

Nobody answered.

"Listen, I'm in a spot of bother." He paused for a minute, allowing them time to process his words. "Do any of you know where I can get a set of false ID?"

No response.

"I'll pay half my wage from tonight to anyone that can help."

The four men looked at one another.

"Who's the guy makes the passports Billy?" Rangers tilted his can at the man who had been the first up the gangplank earlier on.

"The Poet?"

"Aye, that's the one. He still working out of that repair shop in Newcastle?"

"Last I heard."

Rangers looked up at Brad. "Half the money from tonight you say?"

Brad nodded. It was a big price to pay, but it had broken the ice and it was information that he actually needed.

"Remember the name of the place?" Rangers asked.

"Make Do And Mend. Down at Jesmond, not far from the Metro. I've never used him myself, but I've heard good words about his work."

"Perfect. Thanks."

Bumfluff shifted along on the seat. Left just enough space for one more. "While you're up grab us another beer." He crushed his can flat. "Have one for yourself an' all."

Brad went over to the fridge, pleased that he was moving up in the world. He took out a six-pack, caught his balance as *Sriga* hit a big one and joined his new comrades.

*

They made Eyemouth at just before six in the morning. The crew tied up and met below.

Red stood at the head of the table and pulled out a wedge of cash from his bag. He counted out piles and handed them out to the established members. It quickly vanished into various pockets.

"Here's the money for the new lad. Two-hundred quid for your first trip." He passed over the notes and smiled. "If you come along the next time, you'll be on the same rate as the others. If you don't, you didn't see a thing tonight. You weren't here and you've never heard of the name Red. Got it?"

Brad saluted.

"Good lad."

Rangers held out his hand. The rest of the lads cheered. Brad counted out five twenties and passed them over.

He still had enough to feed his family for a week and that meant plenty.

"When's the next trip, boss?" Bumfluff.

"Boris said he could be back this weekend. Reckons he could do twice the runs and still have a queue a mile long. Check in at the Smugglers and I'll let you know. In the meantime, I'll love you and leave you."

Red turned and left the room.

"Anyone fancy a pint?" Rangers looked like he'd had a few too many already.

There were a lot of nods among the group.

"Not today." Brad couldn't wait to get home and see his wife and bairn. "I'll see you at the weekend." He followed Red out onto the deck and took a deep breath. The air was cold and fresh. The gulls above called as if in welcome. He checked the money was safely in his pocket and disembarked.

The ground was solid beneath his feet and the sun was low in the sky. It sure was good to be alive.

*

John Locke was sitting in his car chewing on the last of his Prosciutto di Parma ham ciabatta when Sriga entered the harbour. He licked his fingers clean, turned off the radio and prepared his camera for action.

twelve

Brad and Molly sat at a table outside the caravan site bar, the pint glasses in front of them almost empty.

Shem was playing football on the small AstroTurf pitch with a load of lads who were all bigger than him. The boy was a human dynamo. He never stopped chasing down the ball and went in for every tackle as if he were indestructible. His face was a picture, bright red and shiny with sweat. His glasses had misted and his hair stuck up in countless directions.

"Another drink?" Brad felt the need to wash the taste of the night's work away.

"We said we wouldn't do this." Frown lines buried themselves into Molly's forehead, spoiling her looks for a moment. She looked like a Swedish model this afternoon, two neat plats tied around her head, Brad's favourite style of all.

"We're celebrating. No more being apart."

"We've been raising a toast to that one ever since you went on leave."

"The new job, then. There's money in the kitty again. Let's have another."

There was a clatter on the football pitch as someone smashed into the surrounding fence. Brad saw Shem getting up from the ground and limping back to the game. He was no quitter.

"How was work? You never said."

"I'll get another drink and then I'll tell you everything." Brad got up and walked to the bar without looking back. He ordered another couple of beers and a whisky. He downed the short as soon as it was put in front of him. Let the waves of heat blaze through his body. Paid for the round and returned to the picnic table.

"So tell me what you did on the ship."

"It was nothing much."

"Paint me a picture."

He took a long swig of his lager. Diluted the hard stuff and refreshed his spirits. Rubbed the beard on his chin and ordered his thoughts. "Truth is it sucks."

Molly reached out and touched his hand. "I can see you're worried."

"These guys are into a lot of shit. There's a hold full of migrants just arrived into the country. I reckon they're trading drugs, too. And a load of amateurs are armed with sub-machine guns."

His wife's mouth opened and her lips formed an O of concern.

"Don't worry. I've spent the last five years on a sub around nuclear warheads. I've handled more weapons than these guys have had fish suppers. A few bullets won't scare me."

"Christ Brad. I'm scared enough for both of us."

"It'll be fine."

"Will it?"

"Next trip I reckon I'll bring home a couple of grand. That's what the rest of the crew get for a night's work."

"That's not what I asked."

It was time to tell it as it was. "Then I don't know. I'm used to being with a tight team of well-trained individuals. The navy have always had my back. I don't think there's anyone on *Sriga* who gives a stuff about me."

"I don't like it. You need to quit. Now."

Brad looked over to his son's game. Shem was in goals. A pair of huge gloves covered his hands. There was a look of grave concentration on his face as he followed the action. He clapped a shot at the other end of the pitch and made the noise of flapping rubber.

"But the money's great. I do that a few more times, I can make back the cash I lost the other day. We can get those passports and head south just as we planned and I'll be able to get a proper job. One with health-and-safety and decent hours."

The Shallows

Molly folded her arms across her chest. Brad knew that she was trying to look determined and solid. All he saw was her amazing breasts coming together and forming the perfect cleavage. If they'd been alone he would have dived straight in. "You can't go again. I'm not having Shem losing his father just because of money. It was bad enough having to live without you when you were on a voyage, but at least we knew you'd be back."

His throat tightened. She was right about the risk. The problem was they were in a fix. Two rounds of drinks at the site and a tankful of petrol for the Volvo and they were already a meal out away from having nothing again. What kind of father put his kid through that? A picture of his own dad sitting in front of the TV after they laid him off from the factory flashed through Brad's mind. He wanted to do better than that for Shem. Be a role model his son could be proud of. The navy uniform had done much to help with that, but it couldn't make up for him being gone for months at a time. That wasn't what parenting was about. He needed to do something solid. To bring home enough money to give his son the trimmings he deserved.

"I have to, Mol. We're running on empty and we need cash to get down to your gran's cottage."

Molly's lips trembled and her eyes filled with tears. He had to find a way to put her back together.

"Tell you what. I'll do the next run. Saturday, Red told us. I'll pop down to the Smugglers tomorrow and find out the details. I get paid and you can pick me up at the harbour. We'll leave right then and head straight down to our honeymoon hotel in Grange." He rubbed her hands and leant in. "Then we're on our way to Cornwall. How's that sound?"

Molly bent forward and threw her arms around Brad's neck. Her tears dropped. He felt them land with a warm splash on his chest. He rested his chin on the top of her head. Pressed down and pulled her close. Tried to absorb her pain through his skin as her shoulders bobbed and shook.

thirteen

When the call came through from the hospital to say that David Wong was conscious and out of danger, Shanks was just finishing a rather delicious cooked breakfast in his hotel dining room. The doctors said their patient was ready to be interviewed as long as he wasn't pushed too hard. Shanks hurried the last of his coffee and toast and went to his room to collect his jacket and his bag.

He swung by the station to pick up Hawley and they arrived at Wong's bed before nine. They didn't know each other well enough to decide how they might work any good-cop/bad-cop routine. Agreed to improvise and see where it got them.

Hawley pulled up a chair and sat down. Shanks remained standing.

"Come on David." Shanks pinched Wong's big toe and gave his foot a shake. "We can tell you're awake. Your eyeballs are shaking."

Wong opened his eyes a fraction and blinked away the light. He had a broad face and jet black hair that flopped over his forehead in an unclean fringe. His face was pale and his lips thin. At the opening of his gown was a chaotic scar that pulled tight at the skin below his neck and suggested a burn or a scalding of some sort. A tube was taped to his arm and wound its way to a drip attached to the frame of the bed.

Hawley took out his phone and made a big show of setting it up to record the conversation. He put it on the table next to him and removed a leather wallet from his pocket. "It looks like you've got yourself all better to find yourself in a knot of trouble. I'm Sergeant Hawley of Police Scotland." He flashed his ID badge and looked up at his new partner. "This here is Captain Shanks, working for the Navy over at Faslane. It's early and neither of us is in the mood for this. When we ask you questions, your answers need to be straight as the crease in Shanks's trousers."

The Shallows

Shanks prickled at the reference to his appearance. He curled his fingers into a fist, squeezed hard and relaxed. "Obviously we're sorry you got shot and everything, but we need information. Like, when did you start working on the plantation?"

"I'm unemployed." Wong struggled to lift his body from the pillow, reached out to his bedside table and found nothing.

Shanks made him as a smoker. A good sign. Addicts usually broke quickly. They might not have to stay on the ward for as long as he had first feared. "Then can you tell me why you were out in the wilderness in the company of a hardened criminal playing with guns last Sunday?"

"I was sightseeing."

"It was the middle of the night."

"Junior and I, we like the stars. There's no light pollution in the hills."

"It was pissing down with rain. The clouds were thick as Marmite."

"We're optimists."

"Really?"

"And we had umbrellas."

Hawley leaned in. "Of course you know that Junior didn't make it." From the look of surprise on Wong's face, it was clear he hadn't been told.

"So, you went up to the old house to wait for a break in the weather and you stumbled into a drugs operation. Is that how it went down?"

"You're good at your job. That's exactly how it was."

"And whoever was there already didn't take kindly to having visitors. They came out to scare you off with a few warning shots."

"Yep."

"Only they didn't know how to use a gun and took out you and Junior by mistake."

"It's like you were there, officer."

"Next thing, you're waking up in this place getting your meals from a plastic bag."

"Exactly."

Hawley looked up at his partner. "You see, I told you there'd be an innocent explanation. The man knows nothing."

"You're forgetting a couple of things Sergeant."

"Oh?"

"The fingerprints."

"Ah, yes. I forgot to mention. While you were at death's door, we took the liberty of grabbing a set of prints. In the interest of finding your medical records, of course."

"And the funny thing is that they matched with those we found in the barn. They were everywhere. On the drugs, the tools, the guns. You name it and we can pin you there."

Wong sagged at the news. He suddenly looked a size or two smaller.

"The game's up." Hawley sat back in his chair, unbuttoned his jacket and crossed his legs. His open posture spoke of victory. "All you need to do is to decide which side you're on. Do you want to play with the good guys or stay with the darkness?"

"I don't know anything."

"What's the matter?" Time to bring out the big guns. "Are you scared that Red will find out?"

No answer.

"What you say here, I promise it stays between us. I'm more interested in the shooters than the cannabis. I leave that kind of thing to the drug squad. They're not as nice as we are. Too many years spent undercover if you ask me. All that pretending goes to their heads in the end."

"So tell me how it went down and I'll see if we can cut you some slack when it comes to the charges." Shanks pushed Wong's legs to the side of the bed and sat down.

"Jesus." Wong winced with pain. "Nurse!" The shout sounded hollow in the acoustics of the room. "Nurse."

"You could try pressing this." Hawley held out the emergency button for a second then pulled it away and kept it in his lap. "But it'll do you no good. I can ask the constable on the door to come in and help. He'll have his first aid certificates. It's part of the job."

"Bastards."

"We are. That also comes with the territory."

"The doctors tell me you're a lucky man." Shanks applied a little soft soap. "That bullet had hit you a centimetre to the right or left, you wouldn't be here to talk with us now. If I were you I'd ride that luck. We're the best chance you've got of being out on the streets this decade."

The dark eyebrows on Wong's face knitted together.

"And if you don't, the next time we meet it's likely to be in the prison hospital. I hear the food's shocking in there. Not to mention the bed-baths. Rumour has it they have the inmate volunteers doing those."

Wong shook the concern from his expression and nodded. It appeared that his decision was made. "Junior and I were posted out at the farm. All we had to do was tend the plants. Water and feed them. Harvest the crop and bag up." He talked fast, like he needed to get it all out at once. "Someone would show up every couple of weeks and take some of the stock for distribution. The other part of the job was protection. We were supposed to keep everything safe in case the word ever got out."

"And on Sunday night?"

"The job was lucrative and it had its perks, but it was pretty lonely out there just the two of us. When we did get company, it was always men."

Hawley thought about the submariners and how their situation wasn't that dissimilar. And he knew well what it was like to be kept away from women for long stretches of time. It could drive a guy nuts. Maybe it's what had happened to Richardson back on Blue Watch. "And you needed some female company."

"Exactly. At first we went out one at a time. That way there was always someone around protecting the investment. Then we realised that nobody was likely to stumble into us unannounced. Have you been there? It's a butt-hole of a place."

"The tourists seem to love it."

"They can't get enough of the Jimmy hats either." He fingered the scar tissue under his gown. "Anyway, we took to going out at weekends. Just Saturday nights at first. Then Fridays. This was our first Sunday off the premises. I guess we were getting a taste for the girls. They were hot like Szechuan."

"Their names?"

"We weren't monogamous."

"From that night."

"I think it was Shelly and Trix."

"We'll find them where?"

"Down at the Fiddler's Elbow in town."

"So, you had your way with these two fine ladies and you were back to base at what time?"

Wong shrugged. "Must have been after eleven."

"What was different when you came back?"

"There was this car out front."

"Colour?"

"We already established it was dark. It looked black. Could have been anything. We park up and get out and this guy comes out saying he's been camping and they're looking for shelter from the rain."

Shanks took a plastic wallet from his bag. He slid out a picture of Bradley Heap. "This the guy?"

Wong squinted. "Could be. If you added a beard and a couple of years. Yeah, I think that's him."

"You'd never seen him before?"

"Correct."

"And then what?"

"It was tense at first. Then the man in the photo told his story about what had happened up at the loch and we relaxed a bit."

"But the mood didn't last."

"Not for long. There was a kid in the car. He said something about his mum. They hadn't said anything about her before and it didn't sit right. Junior went for his gun. Before he got it out of his jacket, there was a flash and a bang and he was lying on the floor all bent out of shape."

"You decided to stay behind and fight for his honour."

"I'm not stupid. I was out of there. I ran the way I came in."

"Only you weren't fast enough."

"I was quick, believe me. The bullet just beat me, that's all."

"And it was the man in the picture I showed you who killed your mate and nearly put you in a wheelchair for the rest of your life?"

Wong looked puzzled. "The woman did the shooting."

This was a left field moment. Shanks needed a second to refocus. He took out his iPad, turned it on and located the folder of pictures he'd taken of Heap's flat. It didn't take long for him to find what he was looking for, a wedding photo he found stuck behind the wardrobe in their bedroom. He tilted the screen over to Wong. "This the lady in question?"

"Could be. It's hard to tell on account of her looking so sweet and happy." It was true what he said about the image. Mrs Heap's smile was beautiful. Her groom stood tall and proud next to her. He held his hat under his arm as they walked from the church through a guard of honour, two lines of sailors holding their swords high. "The woman I'm talking about had the face of a shark."

That was the thing about mothers, Shanks thought. It didn't matter how nice they were or how gentle, threaten their young and they turned into wild animals with sharp claws and pointy teeth. He'd seen it in his own wife on many occasions before she split with his kids, though by the end of their time together she was permanently spiky.

"Now that wasn't so bad, was it?" Hawley switched off his recorder and popped the phone back into his jacket pocket. "You've been a great help. If you think of anything else that you've missed, make a note of it and tell the constable at your door you need to speak to us."

"Next time we'll bring grapes." Shanks gave Wong's legs a hard slap and followed his partner out of the room.

fourteen

Friday evening. Locke went into the meeting room with the folder of photographs under his arm. He hoped it wouldn't last long. He planned to meet up with Doreen at half-eight in the curry house and was determined the job wasn't going to ruin another potential lifeline. He was dressed in his finest Harris tweed jacket, had a handkerchief neatly folded in his breast pocket and had set his moustache with mango wax for the occasion.

Shanks and Hawley were sitting at the desk. Each of them had an iPad, a phone and stacks of paper. Surrounding them were boards crammed with information about the intertwined cases. In between them, a bowl of sweets.

"There's been a spot of bother I'm afraid." Shanks looked troubled. Maybe something had come up at the interview.

"Oh."

"I heard from base today. The Ministry of Defence has been in touch with my superior, Commander Briggs."

"Sounds serious." Locke put his folder down, sat and took a sweet from the bowl.

"Turns out our Lieutenant Heap has contacted the press."

"So?" He popped the sweet into his mouth. It was sour as hell. Sucked up all his saliva and shrivelled up his tongue. He spat it into his palm.

Hawley and Shanks laughed and high-fived.

Locke chucked the sweet as hard as he could at Hawley's head. He ducked and it hit an image of the dead Sammy Davis smack bang between his eyes.

"Bastards." It was gruffer than Locke had intended it to sound, but he was past caring. At least it wiped the grins from his colleagues' faces.

Shanks straightened his tie and his back. "It's what I feared from the off. That Heap is on some kind of mission."

"Tell me again about the air he's putting into this whistle-blowing."

"On his last voyage, a young midshipman called Richardson decided he couldn't wait to get home to his fiancé to have sex. He slipped into the bunk of another sailor. I'll leave the rest to your imagination."

Locke didn't want any of that in his mind. He waved the story on.

"It was his first time and he had a meltdown. He spoke to Heap in confidence. Heap reported it to the Captain. Told him the guy was in bits. That he was overwhelmed by self-loathing and guilt at having done it with a man and betraying his woman."

"Perfectly understandable."

"Heap did his best to settle Richardson down. Suggested he put it out of his mind and they said a prayer together asking for forgiveness. The next shift everything was fine. Everyone turned in for the night. Richardson never got out again."

"Overdose wasn't it?"

"Yes sir. And that should have been the end of it."

"Except that Heap couldn't cope with the guilt either. He decided to split and that's where you came in."

"Precisely. He wrote a duplicate of his report and has sent it to just about every newspaper in the country. There's also a personal statement imploring the press to take action."

Locke scratched his head. The sour taste of the sweet lingered in his mouth. "I'm not sure I see the problem here."

"The issue of sex in the navy has always been delicate."

"But there are openly gay sailors these days, right?"

"Only they're still not allowed to have sex on the job."

"What about women? Any on this voyage?"

"Not on Blue Watch. There was one. I forget her name. She's on maternity leave right now."

"Surely the MoD have ways of supressing this kind of story."

"They've used their connections and their weight to silence most of the big guns. They've got no traction with the labour-leaning press, though. They don't even bother to contact them. The only good news is that they wouldn't expose anything without doing a huge investigation first. That buys us time."

"Sounds like a lot of fuss about nothing if you ask me."

"With all due respect, sir." Locke's shoulders tensed at the words. "Issues of national security are never to be taken lightly."

These bloody navy boys. They were always so full of it. Perhaps the chefs put something in the cornflakes that inflated their egos.

"He's right, John." Hawley had that same self-confidence. They probably added something to the porridge at the public schools, too. "We need to track the guy down and get to him before he has time to do any more damage."

Locke's moustache prickled against his skin. It twitched up on the right-hand side. "That, in case you hadn't noticed Sergeant, is what we're bloody well doing here. It's what they pay us for."

"And we're earning our corn. You've nothing to worry about on that score."

"I saw the notes from the interview. Are you confident this Wong fellow is reliable?"

"One hundred per cent." Hawley looked at something on his screen. "The killer was the woman, I'm certain of that. Wong has no reason to lie."

"We've already alerted the media. They'll be running with pictures of Molly Heap tomorrow morning. I've also got an artist's impression of how Brad Heap might look with his beard and it's doing the rounds as we speak." He pressed the screen of his iPad a few times and turned it round so that Locke could see it. "Here."

Locke's heart bounced like a rubber ball on concrete. It was a face he already knew. The only thing that was missing was the earring. "I should've bloody well known." He opened up his own folder. Threw down the photographs from his morning at Eyemouth Harbour. "Feast your eyes."

They did, flicking through the pile and studying hard.
"It's him all right. Nice work John."

"Nice?" The word was pitched at an octave higher than Shanks usually managed. "You had our man in your sights and let him go?"

Even though Locke wanted to slap the sailor, he knew the man was right. Brad Heap had been in his view and Locke had done nothing.

Hawley pointed down at the shot of the van with the immigrants getting into the back as if they were just popping out for the day. "Doesn't look like they're catching fish out there, John."

"There's no money in that anymore."

"It doesn't make sense." Shanks looked puzzled. "How does a sailor based at Faslane manage to get tied up in drugs and illegal immigration and Lord knows what else? He simply wouldn't have the time."

"Ours not to reason how. The pieces are coming together nicely. My assumption that Brad had nothing to do with the cannabis plantation was clearly wrong." How he hated to admit it. "We don't know if Brad just stumbled into the work or whether he's related to Red. That's not important. What we have is your whistle blower stepping over to the dark side."

"The man was a serious Christian." Shanks. "That's why he spent time with Richardson. It was part of his duty down there."

"They're always the worst. Scratch the surface and there's a demon inside just waiting to spring out and stretch its legs." A plan was forming as Locke spoke. All he needed was to keep it in mind before it vanished. "You should be delighted. Your whiter-than-white Lieutenant is suddenly the devil. Whatever story he's been spreading we can totally discredit."

Hawley nodded. "He's right you know. It's a gift horse and there's no need to count the teeth."

"The main thing is we have it all. This boat goes out every weekend. It's always back within twelve hours."

"Brilliant." Shanks finally seemed excited. "We wait for them to turn up next time and swoop. I pick up Brad, he leads you to Molly and Red Fenton gets tangled up in the net as a bonus. I'll let the commander know."

Locke's moustache twitched again. Same side. "That's not how it plays out. I've been after Red for years. If we're going to do this, I want him caught in the act."

"Red-handed?" Hawley looked very pleased with that one.

"Aye. If you like."

"Then we pick them up at sea. I'll arrange to have patrol ships in the area and we take down the whole operation. If we catch them picking up the migrants, we get the guys at the other end, too."

"You think we're going to follow them out and spook them? No bloody way. We don't touch them till they're back on land. Our team will be waiting for them when they dock. The harbour's perfect. There's nowhere to run and nowhere to hide. All I need to do is to make sure we know when *Sriga* goes out again and we gather the troops."

"Genius." Hawley slapped the table hard.

Shanks didn't seem so sure.

"You go and tell your commander the plan. In the meantime, call off your dogs at the press. Keep those photos on ice for now. We don't want to spook anyone at this stage."

The captain made a show of looking at his watch. Pulled a face like he'd just sucked one of the sour sweets from the bowl. "It's eight o'clock. The first run will have gone already for most of them."

"Jesus." Locke stamped his foot. Damn these navy boys and their brutal efficiency. "They see the pictures, we might lose our edge." If Red Fenton slipped through his fingers this time, he was going on the sick.

"I'll do what I can. We can pull the plug on the later editions. Maybe we'll even catch a few of the early ones."

"You do that. Send me a text when you know where we stand. Hawley, you make sure we've got a team ready for pick-up. They'll need to be on call over the weekend if I've understood the pattern."

"Will do."

"Find out what resources your commander's prepared to spare. If he's with us, get the boys down to Eyemouth as soon as they can make it."

"Yes sir."

"Now if that's all, I'm out of here." He collected his photographs, slipped them back into the file and left it on the table. He smoothed his jacked down, took out his moustache comb and went to leave the room.

Hawley picked up the bowl of sweets. Held them out.

Locke stared down at them. Resisted the urge to bury his comb into the middle of Hawley's head and walked out of the door for his hot date.

fifteen

Molly sat on the stool in the caravan. Her eyes were screwed tight and knuckles white.

The scissors were shaking in Brad's hands.

Molly's hair was perfect. Always clean and silky. He could tell so much about her mood from the style she wore or the way she played with it. When they made love he tangled his fingers in there. Chopping it off would be a betrayal of sorts. As if he was stealing her identity.

"Get on with it can't you? The suspense is making me ill."

Shem walked over and stood by his dad. "Want me to do it?"

Brad looked down at his son. The boy wasn't fazed by anything. "It's all right. I can manage." Even though Shem had a huge heart, those tiny hands weren't up to the job.

"You'd better." Molly was losing patience. "Or I'll do it myself."

What choice did he really have? The photograph of Molly in the newspaper came from her Facebook page. The selfie she had taken on their trip to London. Her hair shone in the sun like a beacon and made her stand out from the crowd. If they didn't get rid of it now, someone would recognise her. She was responsible for the shootings up north. The journalists described her as a loose cannon not to be approached under any circumstances.

The picture was a good one. She would be spotted within hours if they didn't change her appearance. Brad hadn't run away from the navy to lose her now. He opened the scissors and chopped.

The first bunch fell to the floor. They were already past the point of no return.

"I should have killed them both." It sounded like she meant it. "Then there wouldn't have been any witnesses."

/ "You couldn't Mum." Shem sat on the carpet and picked up the hair. "You shot those men because they were going to kill Daddy. That's okay. If you'd shot him again when he was injured, that would just be murder."

The adults didn't answer.

The only noise in the room came from the swishing of the blades.

sixteen

The Heap family treat had emptied the bank. It had been worth every penny. A Chinese takeaway and a sticky toffee pudding with custard satisfied them all. The beers had washed it down nicely. Things had all been going well until Molly mentioned that it was like the Last Supper and burst into tears.

She was crying a lot these days, ever since they decided to try for another baby. They'd be okay though. Would land on their feet in the end. The money would be topped up by morning and they'd be off to their fresh start. They'd find work. Settle down. Conceive and move on. It would be like the miscarriage had never happened.

He pictured Molly with her new black crop of hair as the ship bobbed up and down towards its destination. Hoped she was sleeping soundly and was at peace.

"Wakey wakey, rise and shine." The skipper's voice came through the speaker loud and clear.

There was a lot of moaning from the guys in the bunk. Brad didn't bother to hang around to make small talk. He took his life jacket, fixed the clips and went up on deck to get to work.

He walked over to the wheelhouse and stepped in. "Same as last time Skip?"

The skipper didn't take his gaze from the screen.

"That's right, son." Red slapped Brad hard on the back.

He turned to leave and noticed a newspaper in the pocket of the jacket hanging from the door. It looked like *The Sun*. The one with his face plastered over the front cover. It didn't matter that the artist's impression of his beard was terrible. Anyone who paid attention would see the likeness. It worried him that he was on the verge of being exposed. Not that these guys would care that he was on the run. What he didn't want was to let Red and his gang get any leverage over him. Reduce his pay or blackmail him. He was in enough trouble already. "Mind if have a read of your paper?"

The Shallows

"Yes I do." Docherty still didn't turn around. "I'll want that on the way back home when I'm having my mug of tea. Leave it where it is. I finish it before we're done, you can have it."

There was no more time to discuss the matter. The ships were coming together.

Red pushed him out of the door. "You need exercise lad. Try lifting a few of them tyres over the side."

"I'm on it." Brad walked over to the rail and set to work.

The rest was an action replay of the night before. The guns. An exchange of bags. A steady stream of grateful migrants off to shelter in the hold. The parting of the ways. It may have been strictly illegal and dangerous, but there was nothing exciting about it. Brad was bored to the point of exhaustion. By the time he finished his work, all he wanted was to sleep. He wandered down below, didn't bother to remove the life jacket or his immersion suit and wrapped himself up in one of the spare blankets.

Next he knew he was being shaken awake. "Get up." It was Rangers. His face was serious and cold and he wore an Uzi over his shoulder. Adrenaline pumped through Brad's system and made him alert. All those years of training and working on the sub meant his body could turn itself on before his mind caught on. He was up on his feet and ready to move when he registered that this was all wrong. "Red needs to see you. Soon as."

Brad wondered what he could have done. The migrants all made it on board and he tied the ships together perfectly. It had to be something else.

He walked up onto the deck and looked up at the stars. They were beautiful. Like a million eyes staring down and watching over him. He fingered his cross and hoped his guardian angels were paying attention.

Rangers gave him a shove. Brad stumbled towards the wheelhouse and went in.

The greeting was swift. He saw the swing of an arm. The cartilage in his nose crunched under the weight of the fist that hammered into it. The spark of pain soon became a furnace. He found himself sitting on his arse, back against the wall and looking up at an angry Red.

"You prick." Red's face was the colour of his name.

Brad shook his head. His brain fluid sloshed around inside his skull. He tasted the iron in his blood as it trickled down his throat. Nothing was making sense.

Docherty picked his newspaper and held it out for all to see. The front page carried the pictures of Brad and Molly. It might be the last time Brad set eyes on his wife and son. He wanted to puke but fought the urge and pushed himself up from the floor. His knees were too weak to lock, so he leant back against the wall to keep upright.

"You believe in fate, lad?"

He used to. Now he understood that life was about the decisions you took. You made your bed, you lay in it.

"Well I'm starting to. How else can you explain it? A couple walk into a very lucrative operation of mine and shoot up the place. They kill one of my old mates. Come within inches of paralysing another of my men."

The words spun around in Brad's mind. He focussed hard. Caught the moment. Understood why his nose was crushed.

"Normally you wouldn't expect to see that couple again. If they had any sense they'd bury themselves deep underground. Instead of that, one of them walks into my pub and I offer him a job. What are the chances of that?" Red shook his head. "It's a miracle. There's nothing else it can be."

The whole thing sounded ridiculous. Brad suspected that he was really still asleep and wrapped up in his blanket in the cabin, trapped in a nightmare. Things like this didn't happen in real life. It was almost impossible to believe.

The Shallows

The slap of Docherty's hand against his cheek hurt far too much to be part of a dream and snapped him to attention. "It was a mistake. A misunderstanding. We didn't mean any harm. All we wanted was a place to stay out of the rain." This wasn't going well. He needed to calm himself. Work out his options and commit to making a choice. He looked around the room. Weighed up the strength of the opposition. Two hard men, one old sea-dog and an Uzi for starters. Another three crew members down the stairs to back them up. The odds weren't good.

"I've half a mind to keep you alive and set David Wong on you when he gets out of hospital. He's a master in the art of the slow and painful death."

"Don't be stupid." Docherty clearly wasn't impressed by the idea. "We do this now."

Rangers slipped the strap from his shoulder and took the gun in his hands. Brad's heart beat a little faster. He checked the room for objects he could use. Docherty's mug. A small beer bottle. The leather holdall Red had taken from the other ship. None of them ideal weapons.

"He's right boss." It was two against one. Time was running out. Brad thought of his wife and child waiting at the harbour to pick him up. Their lives together as a family flashed through his mind. He needed to get back to them. Had to stay alive. Needed to act while he still had his strength. His arm shifted. He flung it backwards as hard as he could. His elbow caught Rangers on the jaw. There was a crack as bone hit bone.

As Rangers fell into the wall Brad was already shifting his own weight. He reached down, picked the holdall up by the handles and raised it up behind him.

Red was slow off the mark. Brad swung the bag in the biggest arc he could manage. He pulled it upwards and cracked Red in the face. He went down like a cow in a slaughterhouse.

Docherty shouted into his microphone.

Brad didn't bother to process the words. He turned and opened the door. Stepped out onto the deck. Ran hard to the side of the boat and clambered up the rails. He looked into the blackness beneath and then back at the wheelhouse. It was literally a case of being trapped between the devil and the deep blue sea. The decision was a no-brainer. He lifted his crucifix to his lips, kissed it and jumped into emptiness. The air screamed as it rushed past his ears and then he plunged into silence.

He hit the sea hard. Jolted and sank into the depths. Panic gripped him as his senses shut down and his world got further and further away. He thought he would never stop sinking. His lungs tightened as the cold consumed him like some virulent cancer. Saltwater entered his nose and stung the lining of his nostrils. He kicked his legs hard to resist the descent. Held out his free arm to increase the resistance. His body slowed to a halt. He wondered if he had enough air inside him to make it back to the surface alive.

There wasn't time to worry. He began to rise. The rate of his acceleration took him by surprise. Before he could think of anything he could do to help himself his head popped up above the waves. He sucked in oxygen and grabbed tightly onto his bag. His head throbbed in the freezing night air and he hung inside his life-jacket like a limp doll.

A light passed over a nearby wave and brought Brad to his senses. It seemed an age since he took the plunge and yet *Sriga* was only fifty metres away. He could see a beam shining from the back of the ship, piercing the darkness and circling the area. Behind the lamp, the dark silhouettes of angry men, arms pointing this way and that.

Over the howl of the wind and the throb of the engine he heard the scream of gunfire, short bursts of sound ripping the air apart.

Brad shifted his weight onto his back. Kicked his legs like a frog, urging them to put distance between himself and his pursuers. Years of training had taught him that finding a body in the sea was a difficult job even in the daylight. All he needed was to keep swimming and try and stay calm.

The Shallows

The boat was turning. With each second it was shifting further away. Brad kept his legs moving.

The noise of the engine disappeared. The wind sang as it pounded his ears. He imagined there were words to the chorus. Tried hard to find their meaning. There was none.

As *Sriga* vanished from view, Brad realised that he was totally alone. The only people looking for him wanted him dead. The rest of the universe barely knew he existed.

seventeen

John Locke surveyed the scene below. To the passer-by, everything would look as it should. Just another early morning at the harbour, the gulls keen to start their day and a few folk walking their dogs along the front.

Beneath the tranquillity, Locke knew there were teams of men prepared for action. He thought of them as tightly coiled springs primed to unleash their energy into the world.

The huge white van parked on the street contained a unit of police officers dressed and ready for battle. An armed response team was resting up in a small family cruiser moored to the sea wall. The navy had come up trumps and thrown in a crew who were currently nestled inside the cabin of one of the trawlers. Two more vans were laid up on the edge of town awaiting the call. Hawley and Shanks were in their car just in front of Gunsgreen house.

Locke was sitting on a bench, smoking a cigarette and sipping coffee from his flask. He was tired and hung over from the night before. The caffeine wasn't helping. Nor was the fact that *Sriga* was late. His muscles were tight and needed to move. He stood up and went to look out to sea again.

Nothing.

If the buggers didn't show soon, he'd have to make a decision. Whether to keep everyone poised or to stand them down. Calling it off would see him losing face. There'd be a dressing down from his superiors. A slamming of the overtime bill and the heavy-handedness of the operation. Another blot on his copybook in a world where paperwork was supposed to gleam white.

Not that he cared that much what they said. Going after Red was important. Meant he could hang up his badge knowing there was one fewer loose end. If he was given a rollicking in the process, then so be it.

The Shallows

The sight of the waves helped him find focus. He thought of Doreen back at her cottage, all snug in between the covers, her heavy breasts melting into the mattress, the love bite blossoming on her neck.

His phone buzzed inside his pocket. He took it out and clicked on his new message.

'Target approaching port. Estimate twenty minutes to base.'

He punched the air, flicked his cigarette butt down onto the beach below and skipped back to his bench to prepare for action.

eighteen

Seven o'clock in the morning. The boot of the Volvo was packed to the top. Shem shared the back seat with a suitcase and his teddy bear. He was using his toy binoculars to look out of the window, hoping to get a glimpse of his dad coming home.

Molly checked her hair in the rear view mirror. It was a God-awful job that Brad had made of it, but the more she saw the rough cuts and wildness the more she liked the style. It was primitive and carefree and made her feel adventurous.

What lay ahead of them, she couldn't foresee. Whatever it was, she would embrace it. They could be a proper family now that her husband had quit his navy life and as long as they stayed together she didn't care about the rest.

Soon as Brad came ashore, they were heading south. She reckoned it would take four hours to drive down to Grange. A few days there and then on to Cornwall and her gran's cottage. They could stay there until mid-September. That gave them a few weeks to get their act together. When Gran got back, they intended to go to Spain. Spend the month in the heat and save up some money. As long as they had the false papers they could travel anywhere after that. Paris. Barcelona. Rome. The world was theirs for the taking.

"It's Daddy's boat." Shem sat up in the back and focused the binoculars. "He's home. I'm going to meet him." Shem didn't wait for instructions. He opened the door and set off running along the promenade. Molly was happy to let him go. The boy had been cooped up in the car for almost an hour. He might as well get some exercise while he had the chance. She watched him jog all the way around, over the bridge and onto the other side. By the time he was there, *Sriga* was pulling up against the harbour wall.

The engines went into reverse and the back of the boat swung in. The men on deck stood ready with ropes. They threw them over the bollards like skilled cowboys lassoing cattle.

The Shallows

Molly's heart raced as she waited to greet her husband. It was always the same when he was out at sea, a relief to see his feet touch dry land.

Shem was standing against the far wall watching. He looked over to Molly and gave an enormous wave.

Molly was about to wave back when chaos poured down onto the scene. The back doors of the white van by the basin burst open and a mob of police ran out towards the boat screaming.

Another group of men in navy fatigues spilled over from a neighbouring boat onto *Sriga*. Two vehicles sped along the road with sirens hooting like unhappy alarm clocks.

It was pandemonium.

Molly's first concern was Shem. She looked through the action and saw him standing still, body pressed into the wall and arms by his sides. When she knew he was all right, she focussed on the boat.

The uniforms swarmed over the decks and pinned down each of the crew in turn. Four rough looking men allowed themselves to be cuffed without offering resistance.

A large red-haired man and an older guy wearing a skipper's hat stepped out of the wheelhouse. They held up their hands in surrender.

A heavy bloke in plain clothes appeared, surveying the scene like a general after a successful battle. His moustache was the size of an upturned slice of watermelon. His suit was far too dressy for this time of the day.

The three men came together. They talked as if they knew each other and then the two sailors held out their arms to be cuffed. The general obliged and, acting out the part of perfect gentleman, let them walk ahead as they went to get off the ship.

Policemen disappeared below. Molly expected them to return at any moment with Brad in tow. Instead they came back with nothing.

A chill ran down her spine. She remembered why this was to be Brad's last trip with Red. That the men on board were dangerous. They were involved in serious crime. What if they'd turned on Brad? Found something out about him that they didn't like? Read the newspaper and drawn some bizarre conclusion?

Her breathing was quick and shallow. Her head lightened and she had to sit down on the concrete steps of the promenade. It was as though she had picked up the news from the ether. Her husband was dead and there wasn't a thing she could do about it. Her body sobbed, but no tears came. She wrapped her arms around her shoulders and gave herself a hug.

Next she knew, Shem was by her side. He held on to her and kissed her on the ear. "Don't worry Mum. He must be somewhere else. We'll find him. I know we will."

She grabbed hold of him and pulled him close. Squeezed so hard she almost suffocated the only man she had left in her life.

nineteen

There were no windows in the interview room and Red's sweaty odour had taken over. He sat back in his chair with his arms folded across his chest and stared at the ceiling.

Hawley took out his notebook and pressed record on the machine. His lilac shirt looked crisp and clean, like he'd only just bought it. "It's not looking good for you, Mr Fenton. Your boat's full of illegal migrants and unregistered weapons. We've got your crew locked up along the corridors. They've got plenty to say about what you've been up to, so you might as well just give it up now."

"You reckon?"

Locke would almost have preferred it if Red had adopted his right to silence if it meant the sardine stink from his mouth didn't have to be shared.

"I sincerely do. Any cooperation at this point will leave you in good stead when it comes to a court appearance."

"If we make it that far."

"We'll get there, Mr Fenton. It's just a matter of how soon and what the charges might be."

"Then bring it on."

"I'd like to ask you about the people we found in your refrigeration hold. Seventy-five of them in all. We know you couldn't have made it abroad and back in the time you were out, so it stands to reason someone brought them here to you."

Red put his hands behind his head and laughed. "Typical of you lot to twist things around. A man goes out fishing, does his good deed for the day and ends up trussed up like a criminal. I should be a hero, mate."

Locke's tea went down the wrong way. He spluttered and coughed until his breathing settled. Surely Red wasn't going to try and get off with this. The man was insane.

"What exactly do you mean?" Hawley seemed unfazed by the turn of the conversation.

"You heard. There we were, out in the sea looking for a decent shoal when we see this boat in trouble. It was listing as though it had a heavy load that had shifted to one side. No sailor worth his salt would ignore another craft in a state like that, so I did the only thing I could. I asked my skipper to go over and help."

Hawley loosened his tie and opened his top button. "And then?"

"We tried the radio, but it was useless. They were speaking Russian or something. I didn't understand a word, but the international language of panic in their voices was clear as anything." He gave his nose a pick. "I used my initiative. We tied up together and they lowered a walkway. I got two of my men to secure it. As soon as they were done, this line of Africans came down. You should have seen the grins on their faces. They hugged us like we were gods."

"You were the angels of mercy then."

"Damn right we were."

"I'm impressed by your sense of duty." Shanks looked over to Locke and nodded.

"You rescue a lot of migrants at sea by the looks of it." Locke took several photographs from his briefcase and handed them over to Red. They showed groups of men climbing from *Sriga's* hold and getting into the back of a white van. "These were taken earlier in the week. Were they also from a sinking ship, or is there some other yarn you want to construct?"

Red's expression didn't change. He passed the photos back and leaned in. "What migrants are you talking about? This was a group of tourists we took out the other day. And before you go investigating, I don't carry a licence for that, which might give you grounds to charge me after all."

The man sounded like he believed what he was saying. If they managed to get him behind bars, he'd be a shoe-in for a main part in the prison pantomime.

"I suppose you can explain the machine guns you had in your possession, too."

"The guns aren't ours. They came with the Africans. I didn't fancy leaving them with loaded weapons, so we confiscated them as soon as they joined us. I was planning to hand them in to the authorities when we moored up, only we were attacked by a load of blooming idiots before we could do anything."

Hawley began a slow handclap. "Very impressive. I guess that's what they mean when they talk about a fisherman's tale." He stopped clapping. "The thing is, Mr Fenton, your crew have a completely different story."

If only that were the case. The rest of them were in total agreement with their boss. It must have been an excuse hatched as a contingency plan. They had it practically word for word, right down to the confiscation of the guns.

"Then it'll all come out in court and the jury will decide. In the meantime, I'd like to call my lawyer. He'll need to hear what happened so he can contact his friends in the press. Explain to them how a bunch of brave sailors were wrongfully arrested after their humanitarian feats."

The thought of Red on the front page was too much to bear. Locke turned off the recorder and stood up. "We'll get you all right, you slippery bastard."

Hawley frowned at Locke, switched the recorder back on and picked up his file.

"One last thing." Another set of photographs was handed across the table. These showed Brad Heap getting on board and setting off to sea. "This man you left with, he seems to have vanished from the face of the earth. Would you mind telling me where he went? I've got a very enthusiastic naval officer on the team who has a burning desire to speak to him."

"Brad. Nice guy. I liked him."

"Liked?"

"I only hired him this week. He knew nothing about fishing, but he was good with boats. A qualified marine engineer's always good to have around."

"And what happened?"

"What we did was risky. Tethering two vessels together in the choppy waters isn't the easiest thing to do. Brad was working the ropes. He made a rookie mistake and got himself tangled up when we were separating. The skipper witnessed him go overboard as we pulled away. That was the last we saw of him. Of course we looked, but we couldn't find a happy ending."

Locke's spirits sank. He knew the story wasn't true, but suspected that it was as close to what actually happened as Red was going to get. What they did know was that Brad Heap hadn't returned. If Locke had let Shanks have his way, they would have swooped before Sriga left harbour. Their man would be safely wrapped up. Now it seemed most likely that it would be down to some innocent to stumble across the body washed up on a beach, nibbled at by fish and bloated by the water. Whoever did the finding would have nightmares for years to come. The whole thing had turned into a sorry mess.

"You didn't feel like telling us this when we picked you up." Hawley still had his wits about him. "So we could inform the coastguard and try and save him."

"He probably had a heart attack when he hit the water. It's damn cold out there at this time of year."

"Even so."

"It must have slipped my mind."

The urge to slap Red's face was strong. Locke gripped on to the chair to stop his hands flying. He turned to Hawley. "Turn it off."

"But John, we..."

"Now." There was no point in being in a position of authority if you didn't abuse the power once in a while.

Hawley did as he was told.

Red stood up. "When you get out of here, I want you to take a message to that bastard Gary." His fists were clenched. It was good that he was angry. There might be a chance of cracking him after all.

"I've no idea who you're talking about."

"Sure you don't."

"Hand on heart."

"You don't have one, Inspector."

Locke joined in with the joke. He felt around his chest as if he were looking for a beat. "I'll be damned. You're right."

"Tell Gary I know it was him. I wish I'd finished him off when he attacked my Kylie. That'll teach me to get attached. He was like the son I never had. I was always too soft on him and look where it got me."

"I'll make sure he gets the message." The nerve in Locke's leg twitched. All this sitting down was doing him no favours. Not that he minded. Finding a chink in Red's armour gave a rosy glow to proceedings. It was a fine place to finish for now. He let Hawley hold the door for him and left Red to the uniforms.

"How are we doing with the immigrants?" To Locke it seemed that they offered the most useful point of attack.

"Not well. They don't know a word of English between them and we've only just established they're from Syria. All our translators are down south and overseas. We have to wait until tomorrow afternoon to get anyone up."

There was no point sweating about it. This kind of thing was typical. Hanging around for some specialist or other to travel north and brave the Scottish climate was commonplace.

"Soon as you have anything, let me know."

"Sure." Hawley still looked like he'd just dressed for a job interview. "But now I'm going home. There's a bottle of wine there with my name on it."

It reminded Locke that there was something waiting for him with his name on it too. The cosy buttocks of Doreen Blake, all ready for another round of action between the sheets. The hint of the pleasures to come warmed his mood. Finding this Gary character could wait until tomorrow.

twenty

Brad could no longer feel his feet. His legs were leaden and were barely working. If it weren't for the lifejacket, membrane suit and the buoyancy of the bag, he would have perished many hours earlier. The shore was less than a mile away. One final push and he felt he could get there.

Problem was his mind was playing tricks, shutting down or disappearing through tunnels into the world of his imagination.

He recited a mantra to himself. At first he had said it out loud. Now that his mouth was dry and sore from the salt in the water, he could only manage to do it in a whisper. He repeated it one more time. "Stay awake. Kick again. Use your arms. Remember how much they need you." His limbs shifted into action and he was that bit nearer to land.

His eyes were heavy and sore. Their lids came down slowly like old metal shutters. He let them get so far down and then forced them up again. It took all his strength to keep them open.

He looked up at the cliffs ahead. They were red and beautiful in the evening sun. If he got there before dark he figured he'd be okay. If he didn't, the cold air and the change of tide would more than likely do for him. He repeated his mantra and mobilised his body one more time.

A few more strokes and he rested his head on the bag he stole from Red. It was comfortable. Allowed him to relax the muscles in his neck for a moment. He pictured a scene in a fast food restaurant. His family gathered round him. A table full of fries and shakes. It was so real. He reached out for a burger. The roll was soft and the filling heavy. He pulled it close to his mouth and prepared to bite. And then it was gone. His stomach cramped in protest. He clenched his teeth and waited for the pain to pass.

He looked back up at the cliffs. Repeated his mantra and kicked on.

twenty one

Shem stroked his mother's hair as they lay in a bundle on the sofa. They were in the caravan huddled in blankets. She had drunk a bottle of wine to steady her nerves, or so she said. By the looks of things it hadn't worked. Her body was shaking even though they had the gas fire full on and the curtains pulled tight.

It was easiest when she fell asleep. At least she couldn't cry then.

While she lay shivering, he tried to focus.

His dad could be dead. All the evidence said that. But Brad Heap was no normal man. He was a sailor. He knew how to look after himself at sea. They trained him to keep calm in crazy situations and they kept his body and mind sharp so that he could do so. If anyone could survive out there, he could.

When Shem thought about the guns he'd seen on the ship, he forced himself to face the possibility that something really terrible had happened. That Molly was the only parent he had left. It was a horrific idea. Every time it came it made him want to vomit.

With his mum in this state, one thing was certain. It would be his job to come up with a plan.

In the morning they'd get up. They'd finish the rest of their provisions to give them strength. There may not have been any money in the kitty, but there was petrol in the car. When she was ready, he'd make her drive. To the hotel in Grange where they'd had their honeymoon. That's what he had heard them say. If his dad was still alive, that's where he would be waiting.

twenty two

"You're a complete arse Shanks." Commander Briggs was on a rant. "An incompetent fool. What were you thinking letting the civilian police take the lead? You had your man right there in front of you. We've even got the damned pictures of him getting on board." He stabbed his finger into one of them. "If every time we had a crisis we waited to see what happened, the people on this island would all be talking bloody German."

His face turned an unhealthy looking shade of scarlet. If he went on much longer, he might have a heart attack. Chance would be a fine thing.

"We've got the Ministry Of Defence on our backs. I've been fending off the press. Blue Watch don't have their minds on the job. None of them want allegations of homosexuality bandied about." He cleared his throat. "Someone there may well have a relationship on the line and it's our duty to protect them. And all you can do is let our absentee slip through your fingers. It's a disgrace. A ridiculous farce."

He seemed to run out of puff with that. "A total farce." This time the voice was quiet, but the rage remained in his eyes. He picked up a paperweight from his table and threw it across the room. It hit the wall and clattered to the ground.

It was as good a time as any for Shanks to be heard. "Yes sir," was all he could manage. This was the way of the world. The higher up the ranks you got, the more bollocks you were able to get away with. Arguing a point only got you into a whole pile of extra trouble.

Briggs took a pipe from the stand. Pointed the mouthpiece into Shanks's face. "Lucky for you it looks like Heap closed the case all by himself when he took an early exit from the trawler. If he hasn't been eaten by sharks or abducted by aliens and you hear of his whereabouts, we'll reopen things."

The pipe lunged towards Shanks's eye. He moved his head back to avoid injury. "Sir."

"We'll keep in touch with the civvies. If they get a sniff of him, you'll be the first to know and this time we'll take the lead. For now, you can return to whatever it is you do when there's no action."

"Yes, sir." Shanks stood. Saluted like he was hailing the queen and marched out of the room.

When the door closed behind him he turned. Offered another salute to the commander. This one only required two fingers.

twenty three

Brad's body had packed in. Nothing wanted to work. He rested his head upon his bag and made himself as comfortable as he could while he bobbed up and down at the mercy of the waves.

It was almost dark. The street lights created an arc of yellow over the town, like a halo protecting those who lived there. Brad took it as a sign. The angels were coming. Not long now and he'd be leaving one world to enter the next. He felt sorry that he'd doubted his God when things went wrong. Faith shouldn't waver and change direction with the winds. It had to remain resolute no matter what happened. He made a final effort to look into the skies. "Thank you," he whispered and then closed his eyes.

It was time to sleep.

Images played on the inside of his eyelids like a movie on a screen. Molly so happy at the wedding. Shem arriving into the world all covered in blood and bits. The first times and the last. The story of his life. The best moments. The parts he wanted to remember.

The pictures stopped. Darkness slipped down over his eyes as if a visor on a helmet was closing and snapping shut.

His body jolted from sleep. Something was grabbing at his legs. He couldn't let it get him. He kicked out hoping to scare it away.

There it was again.

Something hard. It wasn't giving way.

He lashed out with his heel and hit a solid object.

A jarring pain slashed through his leg.

He feared the worst.

And then he understood.

The waves had taken him to land.

He lowered his legs and attempted to stand. They gave way beneath him.

He tried again and his knees buckled.

The Shallows

It didn't matter. A bit more effort and he'd be safe. His arms responded at once, pulling back against the water and stroking him to safety.

A loud noise filled his ears. It took him a while to identify it.

He was listening to the sounds of his own laughter as his happiness poured into the air.

*

First thing he did when he stepped out was to kiss the land. His lips came up covered in sand and grit. He crawled up the incline of the beach dragging his bag behind him.

His instincts told him to get as far away from the water as possible.

He forced himself to move.

At the bottom of the cliff his energy ran out and he collapsed. His face landed on stone. He opened his eyes and checked his surroundings. The mouth of a cave fifty yards away looked inviting.

He forced himself into an upright position. This time his legs held. He wobbled a few times as he fought to find his balance and then stood still. Now he remembered how to stand. He picked up the bag and walked, each step a small miracle.

The cave reeked of piss. Brad had never been so pleased to come across the stink of humanity in his life. At its mouth, the charred remains of a fire surrounded by a circle of stones.

Whoever had been there hadn't made the slightest effort to clean up. Cigarette butts and empty bags littered the floor. Sandwich wrappers and empty beer bottles lay everywhere. There had probably been food at one point, until the gulls came in to have their feast.

The birds weren't able to unscrew lids though. That skill would have to wait for a further stage of evolution. Which was in Brad's favour. Inside a carrier bag there was a half-full bottle of pop. Full sugar.

In the dim light, Brad couldn't be sure that what was inside was the Fanta Orange as described on the label. It didn't matter. He opened it up and gulped as if he were in a race. The fizz caught his throat, but he ignored it and kept pouring. His stomach filled straight away and bloated with gas. An enormous bubble passed its way up through his throat and presented itself to the world as a satisfying belch.

The act expended the last of Brad's energy.

He walked inside the cave. It was as cool there as it was outside. The darkness was sucking the warmth from his flesh. Whatever heat he had left inside, he needed to keep it there. He curled into a ball and waited for sleep to arrive.

Next he knew it was morning. What had happened to him the day before had been no dream. He was damp and every part of his body shook. His organs felt bruised and tender. Though his bones were chilled, his brow was hot. He needed medication. A Lemsip and a nip of whisky would be fantastic.

He grabbed Red's holdall. It had become like an old friend. Maybe it had something he could use. He unzipped it and looked inside.

It was stuffed full of packages wrapped tightly in bubble-wrap. Someone had gone to a lot of effort to make sure they were waterproof and would float. His scalp tingled with excitement.

He took the top one out. Pulled the tape from the edges and peeled off the outer layer.

Looking up at him through the plastic wrap was the queen. His heart pounded at the sight. He removed the final protection and flicked through the bundle. A thick bundle of used fifty-pound notes. And there were more. He licked his finger and flicked through the pile like a bank teller. He counted ninety-nine of them. He had five grand in his hand. His head went light as if it wanted to float away. His flu symptoms had disappeared completely.

He went back to the bag.

It was full of the bricks. He took them out one at a time. Counted them. Twenty-eight, twenty-nine, thirty. He'd never seen so much cash in one place.

The Shallows

A couple more bricks sat at the bottom, these two larger than the rest. He was sure he knew what they were without having to look. Hard drugs. The kind of shit he hated. They were worth a fortune, but he wasn't interested. His decision was instant. He carried them over to the sea and ripped them apart.

He sprinkled white powder into the waves. Poured out as much as he could and threw what was left of the packages into the water.

Something about the act made him uneasy. What if someone was watching? Had seen the money and wanted to take a slice of the cake?

He held his breath and looked around the cliff-tops. There was no one there. Of course there wasn't. Not even the keenest dog-walker would be up at this hour.

He was a very lucky man. He'd survived Red and his gang and a night in the North Sea. The bag contained more money than he'd earned in all his years of service. His good fortune was overwhelming. He dropped to his knees, put his hands together and offered a prayer of thanks to his maker.

twenty four

Molly was angry with the world. Poor Shem bore the brunt of it. When they were packing the car she had shouted at him more than once and he hadn't done a thing wrong. The pressure was getting her down. Brad was dead. She had no money and her hair was ruined. The police were looking for her and her hangover was murder.

Shem was insistent that they go down to Grange. The poor boy was convinced that they would meet Brad there. She couldn't see the harm in it. After all it was on the way to Cornwall and they would never make it down in one go.

All they needed was a little money to help them along. The bowl of Cornflakes and weedy slices of toast wouldn't keep them going. She had to do something.

They drove to the car park down at the sea front. Molly instructed Shem to stay where he was while she went about her business. At least she wouldn't be able snap at him that way.

She walked around the corner until she was just out of her boy's sight and waited for the first passer-by. It was an old man in a suit and flat cap with a Yorkshire terrier running at his feet.

Molly ran her palms over her hair and then held them out. "Excuse me, sir." Her voice was thin and pathetic. "Can you spare some change for…"

"Piss off." The man walked on in a straight line and nudged Molly into the wall.

She bit her top lip and kept herself together.

A tall lady clacked along in elegant high heels.

"Excuse me…"

"Not today."

And the man who came out of the bank who smelled of cheap aftershave and dressed in a nasty suit. "Sorry, no."

The responses she got for the next twenty minutes were all variations on these themes.

She needed a different tactic.

The Shallows

Back at the car, she took a baseball cap from a suitcase and picked up Shem. The pair wandered down the street to the fish and chip shop and stopped in the doorway.

"You try to look miserable. Like you haven't had enough to eat for a while." That wouldn't be too difficult this morning. She bent down, got some dirt on her fingers and rubbed it over her son's cheeks.

"Mu-um." He said exactly the same thing when she wiped him clean with a flannel.

"It's what we have to do to get a little money. All we need is a few pounds to buy something to keep us going."

They sat down and bowed their heads.

Molly watched the shoes of the townsfolk walk by. She saw some of them cross over the road before they got to her. Others sped up as they passed.

A pair of slippers padded along. Molly noted a map of veins just beneath paper-thin skin and a bandage around the calf. Something dropped into the cap.

"Bless you." She laughed at herself for sounding so Victorian. Waited for the old dear to move on and checked the spoils. Five pence. Shit.

Still, it was the first success of the day. Another hundred like her and they could share a small fish supper.

The next man wore well-polished shoes. He strode with confidence. A man of money, no doubt. There was a rattle of change as he approached. Something dropped into the hat.

"Thank you kindly." That sounded better.

"How much?" Shem asked.

She checked their haul. A piece of chewing gum covered in fur and a foreign coin she couldn't identify. The bastard.

She jumped to her feet. Ran along the pavement. Caught up with the man and pushed him hard in the back. He fell forward and turned round. Tipped his head and looked down his nose.

"Filthy scum." He sniffed and spat into Molly's face. The warm goo splattered over her cheek. She couldn't think of a thing to say. The man walked off as if nothing had happened.

Molly stood still and waited for the tears to arrive. They didn't. Instead, a fire ignited in her belly. She stomped back to the doorway, grabbed Shem by the hand and dragged him to the car.

"Stay where you are. I'll be five minutes." She took the gun from the glove compartment and locked the doors behind her.

The newsagent's was the only shop that she'd noticed doing any business, so that's where she headed.

As she walked through the door a bell announced her arrival.

It was a long room. There were toys and cards in the back and some food basics to one side. She took a basket and went to fill it.

The man at the counter carried on reading his newspaper as if she wasn't there. It was perfect.

First the drinks. A selection of cans of pop to keep them going.

From the fridge, a packet of cheese slices and a pint of milk.

At the food shelves she grabbed at random. It was like she was on Supermarket Sweep. Packets of biscuits, a loaf of white sliced, flapjacks and a sponge cake. Hot chocolate sachets and four-packs of baked beans and spaghetti hoops. Assorted crisps and dips to go with them. Being so carefree was thrilling.

The basket was getting heavy. She put it on the floor and looked at the toys. A grey wolf cub Beanie Baby, a bubble mixture and a packet of Minions Top Trumps. They would keep Shem happy.

She chucked them in and found the chocolate stand. It was like paradise knowing she could pick whatever she wanted. Not that she had time to savour the moment. She grabbed handfuls of her favourites until there was no room left.

It wasn't easy getting to the till without spilling anything, but she managed. She lifted it up and dropped it into the space.

The Shallows

"Want any bags?" The shopkeeper was an unpleasant looking man. His gut was so large that when he stood up it rested on the counter. There were patches of dried sweat on his shirt and the hairs on his chest needed a trim. Molly pitied the wife who had to lie under that.

"Please." A few manners never hurt anyone.

"That'll be five pence each."

"No problem. And I'll take a-hundred Silk Cut and a lighter while you're at it." She hadn't smoked since she became pregnant with Shem, but the way things were going it might not be much longer before she tried her next.

The man turned round. He reached up, opened the little door and took out the cigarettes. His shirt rode up and his trousers fell. The crack of his hairy arse made an appearance and a waft of butt polluted Molly's air.

As he filled the bags, Molly wiped the sweat from her palms onto her jeans. Felt the gun press into her back like a bony finger. She looked out of the window and checked that the coast was clear. If anyone came in now, the whole business would become much more complicated. There was nobody there, but that didn't stop her heart from pounding against her ribs.

"That's sixty-seven pounds and thirty-two pence, pet."

She hated being addressed that way. Who the hell did he think he was dealing with? A bloody dog? She reached under her blouse, pulled out her pistol and pointed it in the guy's face. Her grip was tight. The barrel shook. She took it in both hands to keep it steady and spread her feet to find her balance.

"I think not, darling. How about you empty the till and pay me instead?"

The guy didn't move a muscle. He looked back at her like she was a kid trying to steal a packet of gum. "Come on, lady. I know times are hard, but this isn't the way." His bullfrog chin wobbled as he spoke.

"Give me the fucking money." It came out as a scream. She caught a glimpse of her reflection in the drawers hiding the tobacco. Her face blazed red under her untidy black hair. She was almost scared of herself.

"I'm sorry, I can't. It's what..."

A bang exploded in front of her. It hurt her ears. Her arm jolted upwards from the force of the shot. How the hell had that happened? She smelled fireworks and fear.

The shopkeeper didn't look so cocksure any more. He was looking into the hole in the cigarette boxes behind him with his mouth wide open.

"The money."

His shaking hand turned a key and opened the till.

Molly reached in. She grabbed the notes. Stuffed as many as she could into her pocket and threw the rest in with her groceries.

The man's eyes watered. He slumped down against the wall and sat down on the floor holding his chest. The colour had drained from his face and he muttered something to himself.

Molly didn't bother to ask how he was doing. She picked up her bags, left the shop and ran as fast as she could to retrieve her son and to get out of town forever.

twenty five

There were enough rough looking people on Berwick-Upon-Tweed's High Street to mean Brad didn't stand out. A thriving charity shop culture was ideal to help him blend in even further.

He furnished himself with a new suitcase, clean underwear, a pair of second-hand combats, a long-sleeved top and a thick pullover. Even though he could have bought the entire contents of Oxfam and probably the building to go with it, he got a buzz from grabbing a bargain. The old lady who served him became flustered when he pulled out a fifty pound note. She didn't think she had enough change. To make it easier, he took a full-length winter coat from the peg which meant she only had to part with a tenner.

He put all his new stuff on in the changing room and dumped his old gear into the first bin he saw.

His feet hurt from the walk up from Spittal and his shoes were ruined by a night in the sea. He went into Sports Direct. Everything was on sale. He picked up a pair of football socks and a box of retro Puma trainers and went to pay. He handed over another couple of fifties at the till. The hair in his beard itched like hell while the cash was scanned with ultra-violet light. It received the all clear and the transaction went smoothly.

The soles gave a bounce to his step which took the effort out of walking.

He found a cafe and sat in the window to soak up the warmth from the sunshine. Hot soup, a toasted sandwich and a mug of chocolate went some way to comforting him, but the urge to sleep was overwhelming.

The waitress gave him directions to a hotel down by the river. They were easy to follow and it didn't take long to find.

The Swan was old and painted white. A curved window with thick glass panels stood proud from the main wall. He walked into the reception room and pressed the button on the brass bell.

A lady wearing half-moon spectacles came in and took up her place behind the counter. Her black dress was tight fitting and she had an hourglass figure. Must have been a stunner thirty years ago. She looked him over. Brad didn't think she was admiring his physique.

"Yes?"

"I'd like a room please." Talk about having to state the obvious.

"Single?"

"That's right."

"One night?"

"Three." He could always stay for longer if he needed. "And I need a safe."

"Our bridal suite is the only one with its own. For the others we have a deposit box down here for any valuables."

"Then the bridal suite it is."

She took off her glasses and let them hang on their gold chain. "That also happens to be our most expensive accommodation." She added a little extra intonation as she spoke. Reminded Brad of a BBC presenter from a bygone age.

"How about I have it for the week?"

Her face reacted like he'd sprayed her with cold water. "Let me check." She ran her finger down the register. "I can only have you here till Saturday morning. There's a wedding party booked that evening. Sorry."

"Never mind. I'll take it."

"If you could fill in your details here." She placed a notebook in front of him and he began to write. Shem Bailey was the first name that entered his head. His son's first and middle names. The address was bogus. He put a dash where it asked for the registration of his vehicle.

"That'll be nine hundred and thirty pounds. How would you like to pay?"

"Cash." He took a roll from his pocket and counted the bills out onto the counter.

The Shallows

The receptionist's beady eyes peered over her beaky nose as if she were a vulture looking down on a vulnerable beast. This lady was exactly the type who would check the notes. She'd probably go straight down to the bank and have them individually screened. The cow.

He got to a grand and carried on. Added another hundred quid to the pile. Maybe the tip would make her less keen to investigate.

"Why thank you very much." Her cheeks reddened as she handed over the key. "It's on the second floor. The view's lovely. If there's anything I can do, let me know. The safe is in the wardrobe and the instructions are inside. You just insert your own PIN and you're away."

"Great."

"Would you like some help with those bags?" What a difference being a rich man made.

"I'll manage."

"Breakfast's between seven and nine-thirty in the dining room. The restaurant is open until ten this evening."

"Cheers."

"I hope you find everything to your satisfaction sir. Enjoy your stay."

He picked up his bags. They seemed heavier than they had been when he arrived. He walked up the lush carpet and set off up the stairs.

The corridors were tight and dimly lit. They narrowed as he got higher. The sense of confinement made him shudder.

He arrived at his room and pushed the door open. The bright light was dazzling. When his eyes got over the shock, he checked out his new home.

It was lush. The bed was four-poster. On each of the bedside tables there was a small bottle next to an upturned glass and a chocolate heart. Molly would have loved it.

Two large dormer windows looked out to the Tweed. An impressive arched bridge spanned the water.

The wallpaper was unsettling. Swirls of colour in lavish patterns that would make him feel sick if he looked for too long. The furniture was mostly old. There was a desk and chair, a chest of drawers, the kettle and coffee tray and a huge flat-screen TV. The wardrobe was built into the recess and had mirrored doors. Brad went over and checked himself out. His new gear fitted him well, but didn't look so great now he could see the whole package in one. The swelling at the top of his nose and the yellow smears under his eyes didn't help. No wonder the woman at reception treated him so shabbily. Not that it mattered. The bruises would go and there'd be plenty of opportunity to shop when the time was right.

He slid the door back and checked the safe. It was a chunky metal box with a beige finish of a kind he'd used before.

The instructions were easy to follow and he selected Shem's birthday as his security number.

As he unzipped the holdall, his senses fired up and a wave of nervous energy washed through him. He looked around the room checking for unwanted eyes. Switched on the lights and drew the curtains. Locked the door and checked the handle.

His hands shook as he took out the money and transferred it from bag to safe. There wasn't much space inside and it filled quickly. Brad took it all out and removed the bubble-wrap layers. When he put them back, he was more careful with the arrangement. It was an improvement, but half his cash still needed a home. He closed the door, entered the PIN and looked for a hiding place.

Best option would be a loose floorboard.

Sod's law, he was in a hotel where he builders had known their craft. The boards let out occasional creaks as he walked upon them, but they were solid as the rock he slept on the night before.

The next place he thought of was the canopy over the four-poster. The cleaners would never go up there.

Standing on tip-toes on the chair, he just about managed to reach.

The Shallows

When all the money was up top, he checked it out. To the unknowing eye, there would be nothing to see. It would have to do.

He sat on the bed and fell back into the mattress. The duvet absorbed him and hugged his body. He took one of the bottles from the table beside him, unscrewed the lid and downed the contents without pausing for breath. He closed his eyes and rested his head on the pillows. The wine hit his brain all at once, alcohol soothing his soul and shutting down his synapses. He thought about Molly and Shem. Wondered what they were doing. Tried to imagine them in a happy place. In the pool at the caravan site, playing with the floats and the inflatable hammer. A smile crossed his face and then, as if God pulled out the plug, there was nothing.

twenty six

Molly looked into her rear view and watched a black BMW pull up right to her arse and dart into the other lane. It shot past the Volvo into the path of an oncoming lorry. The truck driver hooted and flashed enough bulbs to light up a movie set.

The driver of the Beamer didn't seem to notice. The car glided back onto its own side of the road and zoomed ahead.

Molly made a gun shape with her fingers. Pointed it at the car and fired. The stupid sod deserved to have an accident.

She checked her own speed. A steady fifty-five miles an hour ever since they hit the A1. Last thing they needed was to be pulled up for speeding.

Shem was finishing off a Yorkie bar. Melted chocolate covered his fingers and surrounded his mouth.

She reached into her door panel and felt around for the wipes. They didn't come to hand. She looked down to check if they were where they should be.

A solid bang snapped Molly to attention. The car jerked hard.

"Shit!" Had she just run someone over? Hurting other human beings was becoming a speciality of hers.

She took her foot from the accelerator and jammed it onto the brake. Checked her mirror as they bumped along and veered left. The steering was wrong. She fought the wheel and turned onto a verge that was all spiky grass and uneven ground. The Volvo stammered to a halt. A screaming car horn almost blew her mind.

"You okay Mum?"

Thank goodness he wasn't hurt. She loosened her grip, unclipped her belt and grabbed him up in her arms.

"Yes darling. I'm fine."

The Shallows

She opened the passenger door, climbed over her son and stepped out. The breeze from the sea carried a chill. She pulled her cardigan tight. Saw the cause of the problem straight away. The front tyre was flat. She kicked it hard. Kicked it again. Kept going until the pain in her toes intervened.

"Shit, shit, shit, shit, shit."

Shem poked his head through the window. Looked like he was about to cry.

Molly's anger with the wheel disappeared. She held her son's head and kissed his hair. Soothing words poured out of her. As long as they could stay together, everything would turn out fine.

*

Nobody had shown her how to put on a spare, just like no one bothered to explain how to get fuel into a car. It was ridiculous that you could drive around at seventy miles an hour and not know the first thing about how to look after the vehicle. These things were all about training yourself. A bit like life really, you had to get on with it and work it out as you went along.

Getting the spare out had been tricky enough. They had unloaded all the gear from the back and set it out on the grass. The wheel lived in a hollow under the floor and she broke a couple of nails trying to lever it from its home.

The jack hadn't been too hard to figure out. It had surprised her just how easy it was to lift the car off the ground.

She strained against the tyre-iron trying to get the nuts to budge. Grease and dirt covered her hands and every time she wiped the sweat from her face she knew she left a smear of black. Her fingers were sore and blistered. Her back ached. She prepared for a final effort, sucking in a deep lungful of air and resting her foot on the rubber.

"One. Two. Three." Each fibre in her body joined the battle. Her teeth squeaked as they gritted together. Something definitely moved. The jack gave way and the front of the car smashed into the ground.

Molly threw the iron. It bounced into the field where Shem sat. She grabbed at her hair and pulled, collapsed into a heap and swore at herself.

"Look Mummy." Shem pointed along the road. "There's a police car."

She turned her head. Saw its blue lights. Watched it drive onto the verge behind them. She pushed herself up and went to the glove compartment. If the coppers were here to take her in, she was ready to fight.

She heard the doors slam shut. Glanced over her shoulder. Saw a young lad with a ruddy face and a woman who was taller than him an old enough to be his mother coming her way. Realised in that instant that the guy was somebody's son. Shooting him was out of the question.

She stood up and came out empty handed. Her luck had run out. It was time to accept her fate.

"Morning Madam." The female officer took the lead. Her hair was tied up under her cap, her brows were over-plucked and her makeup lacked imagination. She gestured to the cases and bags of clothes. "You do know that you're not allowed to run a car-boot sale at the side of a main road, don't you?"

The young constable laughed. His joviality confused Molly.

Shem stepped between them. "We had a puncture. Mummy tried to fix it. I don't think she can."

"Is that so?" The man had the accent of a Norfolk farmer. It made him sound friendly. "Well, it happens that I'm an expert mechanic."

"All that tinkering with tractors back in the day."

"Give me a break." He undid his protective vest and rolled up his sleeves. "Let me have a gander at this. Now where's that wrench?"

Shem went into the field, retrieved it and handed it over.

"Cheers bud."

"It's a pleasure."

"If I can't sort this, we'll call it in. Get someone along who can."

"You can do it mister." Shem's tone was full of encouragement. "I know you can."

The copper got straight to work. He sorted the jack and got the nuts off no problem. Took off the old and lined up the new like it was his profession.

The lady looked up at Molly while her partner worked. Tilted her head to one side and narrowed her eyes. "Haven't we met before?"

Molly's chest tightened. She pretended to think. "I don't think so." She certainly hoped not.

"Back in Sunderland maybe? My daughters still live there."

"Never been." A conversation blocker and the truth.

"So by the looks of it you've just been on your hols."

"Aye. To Loch Ness." She saw Shem's eyes widen at her response.

"See the monster?"

"We took our own." She pulled Shem close.

The officers both laughed.

The woman turned. Called back over her shoulder. "I'll be waiting for you in the car then Laptop."

Molly watched her go. The suggestion of recognition was unsettling. If it was anything to do with the robbery at the newsagent's the penny could drop at any moment. Her body needed to run. To burn off some of its nervous energy. Just standing there was killing her.

Laptop carried on with his work. He was going round each of the nuts tightening each one a little at a time. Shem squatted next to him, cuddly wolf in hand, watching every move like he was soaking up information in case this happened again.

Molly chewed at her broken nails. Tried to bite them into an even line. When they stopped on their journey, she'd go at them with a file.

"There we are ma'am. All done."

She could have kissed him. Once for sorting things out. Another for his form of address.

"Thanks a million. It means a lot." She kissed him anyway. Couldn't help herself. It was either that or break down into tears.

"It's nothing. I'm sorry I won't be able to put all your stuff back in. Criminals to catch and all the rest."

"I understand."

He went over to Shem. Crouched down to the boy's level. They did a silly fist pump with a finger wiggle and said goodbye.

The woman in the car hit the horn. Laptop shrugged, picked up his gear and walked back to his vehicle.

They pulled off quickly, the driver staring hard like she was still trying to place Molly's face. Laptop gave a friendly wave and they were gone.

Shem was already dragging the biggest case over to the boot.

*

It was no good. Her nerves were shot. She couldn't concentrate on her driving any longer. They left the A1 at Alnwick, queued up for an age where arched gate only allowed for single file traffic and parked outside the first hotel they came to.

twenty seven

Brad drove into Eyemouth with care. He pulled the peak of his cap right down over his face and kept his head low. It shouldn't have mattered. His new car, a second-hand Micra, had heavily tinted windows that were just about impenetrable from the outside.

The rain poured from the sky and the streets were quiet. The only person out was and old guy on a step ladder removing Herring Queen banners from the lampposts.

It didn't make much sense coming back to their starting point, but Brad needed to try. The chances of Molly and Shem hanging around after they'd packed the car and found him gone weren't high, but better than nothing. Right then, that was good enough.

He took a detour to avoid the Smugglers Inn and arrived at the turn off for the caravan park.

A group of kids on the Astro kicked a ball about. Brad's mind flashed back to when Shem had been there. He couldn't wait to see the little fellow again. To pick him up and swing him around and tell him all about his adventure out at sea.

He entered the one way system, reassured by the familiarity of it all.

At the fork he turned left.

The police had beaten him to it. Three cars were parked next to the static van that had been home. Two officers stood at the door and there were more inside. He pulled up into a space a little further along. The manager of the park sat at the table talking to a large guy with a bizarre moustache and a smaller man who looked like he worked in sales.

The cops had finally tracked them down. Because they were still hanging around Brad reckoned Molly and Shem had got away. He fingered his crucifix. "Let them be all right, Lord. Keep them safe from harm." He kissed the gold and set off back to his hotel across the border.

On the way out of town his attention was drawn to a soggy board outside the newsagent's. It shouted the headline at him. 'Man Suffers Heart Attack In Eyemouth Shooting'. He slowed the car and focussed on the small print. 'Bonnie Goes It Alone'.

"What have you done now Mol?" He stopped at the kerb. Put on his hazard lights. Pulled his jacket over his head and ran into the shop.

He grabbed a copy of The Gazette. Dropped a pound on the counter in front of a lady with a big face and a down-turned mouth and walked out.

The CCTV image of Molly was fuzzy and didn't do her any favours. Her new hairstyle looked crazy, sticking out in all directions like it was trying to get away from her scalp. She had dark rings under her eyes and her makeup had run. If she didn't already look wild enough, the gun in her hand was a clincher.

He didn't bother to read any more. Threw the paper onto the passenger seat, started the engine and drove off, hoping to see a signpost to normality.

twenty eight

Locke and Hawley sat in silence in the briefing room at Alnwick station.

The door opened and in walked a pair of constables wearing short-sleeve shirts. The woman was taller than the guy. Her hair was tied back in a ponytail. Her face looked like a badly thrown pot. It was too bad. From the neck down she looked good to go. Pert nipples. Hips and thighs that had seen enough work at the gym to give them definition.

The man looked like he must have forged his date of birth to get on the force. His cheeks glowed red. It was a start.

"You want to see us?" The woman spoke first. Locke wasn't surprised. "I'm Sergeant Sykes. This is Constable Cropper."

"Laptop, I believe they call you." Locke stared at the officer hard. Intended to intimidate the guy so that he might learn something from all this.

"Yes sir." The man smiled. "On account of me being a small PC."

Hawley laughed at the joke. "We're here to talk about yesterday."

"No worries."

Locke pointed to the chairs. "Sit down. Get your minds in gear. I want to know everything that happened. If you saw a label on her clothes, tell me about it. Is that understood?"

"Perfectly." The sergeant smiled. It didn't suit her. "Only there isn't much to tell. We came across a vehicle at the side of the A1 this side of the Lindesfarne exit."

"It wasn't safe. We stopped and went to sort it out."

"Turned out it was a flat tyre. I decided it would be quicker to change it than get the breakdown team in, so I did."

"And he was quick."

"Always am."

"That's what the girls say."

"I didn't mean..."

"I know you didn't."

The hell was going on? These fools belonged on the stage. Locke had had enough of their routine. "Stop." He punched the table with the side of his fist to emphasise the message. "I appreciate your fine work at rescuing our damsel in distress. Normally I'd throw you a fish. This time it's not quite the same."

"The woman is a murderer." Hawley took the baton. "An armed robber. A loose cannon. Is there anything you can tell me that might help us uncover something we don't have already?"

"Nothing much." They couldn't fault Laptop for his honesty.

"You surprise me. It's all we get on this case. A big fat zero at every turn."

"They were heading south." Sykes.

"Bravo." Locke clapped his hands together. That narrowed the search down to the whole of England. "Keep them coming."

"They had plenty of gear. Cases and that."

"We made a note of the registration."

"Well, half of it. The last three letters. REM. Like the band."

"Colour?"

"Navy blue."

How wonderfully ironic.

"She had a nice arse." Laptop.

Sykes elbowed her partner in the ribs and gave him the evil eye. "You what?"

"I mean she was in good condition. Slender, like. And curvy at the same time."

"Better."

"They say where they were going?"

The uniforms looked at each other. Blank faces. Shaking heads.

"Or do anything unusual?"

More shakes.

"And you didn't put two and two together when you heard about the incident in Eyemouth?"

"Not until I watched the news when I got in for my tea."

Total washout. "What did you have?" Locke couldn't resist.

"Steak pie and chips."

"Well thanks for your help." Hawley stood up. "If anything else comes to mind, make sure you get in touch."

"Will do." The pair stood up. Turned and went to leave the room.

Laptop stopped halfway there. Looked back. "There was one more thing." He squared his shoulders and smiled. "Her scent. *Molecule 1*. Exclusive to Harvey Nichols and Liberty. She may have looked like a poor scrap of a thing, but that kind of perfume, that's for the classy bird that is."

"We'll make a detective of you yet." Locke held open the door. "You might have a nose for crime after all."

"Thank you sir." Laptop's swaggered out of the room. Locke could have sworn the man had suddenly sprouted by another couple of inches.

twenty nine

Molly sat in the hotel bar nursing a glass of red. She had tried hard to change her appearance, flattening her hair with gel and wearing a pastel coloured scarf. Her makeup was thick around the eyes and her lipstick bright pink. Shem had pulled a face when she kissed him goodnight. It hurt to feel his disapproval, but it meant she had done her job well.

She kept her back to the room so that no one would see her face, not that there was anyone to notice. Even the barman had deserted his post to watch the TV.

The wine tasted fruity and light. Exactly what she needed. The kind of stuff she'd usually throw down her neck like pop. When she had money, at least.

She wasn't entirely skint. The newsagent she robbed must have been doing a roaring trade. He handed over the best part of four-hundred quid after she fired the gun. Enough to keep them going for a while. The hotel was paid up for three nights and she still had a chunk of cash, but what she had would barely cover the price of the fuel to get to her gran's. She took a small sip and savoured it before swallowing.

"Quiet tonight isn't it?" A male voice. The man it came from wore a light blue suit and an open necked shirt. His shoes laced up at the sides and shone like they were brand new. "Maybe you've scared off the locals." His accent was southern and suave. She liked it.

"You think the makeup's too much?" It clearly was.

"Not at all. Just making conversation. Mind if I sit?"

It was too weird. Normally she'd have made an excuse or politely declined, but there didn't seem to be any normal in her life just now. This guy hadn't pointed at her and screamed for the police. His hands were clean and his fingers manicured. He was even on the dishy side in a silver fox kind of way. What harm could it do to enjoy this adult company instead of letting her mind spin out of control? "Not if you buy me a drink." She might as well get something else out of the experience while she was at it.

The Shallows

"You're on."

"A large Rioja then. And a packet of crisps. Your choice."

The silver fox walked over to the bar and got in the round. Molly eyed him up as he stood waiting for the drinks. His hips were slim and his shoulders broad. She would have liked a better view of his buttocks, but the flap of his jacket got in the way. He picked up the tray and returned to the table with the grace of an athlete.

"Here we go." He held the tray above his head like a French waiter, put down the glass of wine and a pint and threw a packet of crisps straight at Molly. Her reactions were fast and she caught it in one hand.

"Mature cheddar and chive."

"Cheese and onion, only twice the price."

"My favourite." She smiled up at the man and realised she was flirting. It seemed such a ridiculous thing to do when her nails were ruined and her hair looked like it had spent the day being flattened under a riding hat.

He slipped the tray onto a neighbouring table and pulled out a chair. As he sat, he hitched the legs of his trousers up. It was nice to see a man looking after his appearance that way. He picked up his pint. "Cheers."

They clinked glasses and drank.

"I'm Tony, by the way. O'Malley. IT consultant based in Oxford."

"You're a long way from home."

"The company sent me up here for a jolly. Fat chance of that around here."

"You mean you don't like it?"

"Not until I came into the bar just now."

"And what changed your mind?" She knew the answer. She just wanted to hear it said out loud.

"They have an extraordinary range of ales and a staggering variety of crisps."

"What else could a man want?"

He answered with a smile and looked right at her. His eyes were blue with flecks of brown and grey. He was totally dishy. "When someone tells you their name, it's tradition you tell yours back. It is where I come from at any rate."

"Suzy." The one she gave the hotel. "Mostly I'm a mum."

"Well then. To answer your question. Suzy. That's what a man might want."

Two minutes he'd been there and his cards were already on the table.

"I'm also a housewife. At least I'm the '*wife*' part." O'Malley didn't show any signs of caring. "Or I used to be."

"And you've been alone since?"

Her eyes filled up and she looked up at the ceiling. The cornice was an elaborate piece of work in need of a dusting. She downed the remains from her first glass. "Yesterday." The tears skated down the side of her nose and blobbed onto the table.

"I'm sorry." O'Malley seemed sincere. "If I'd known I'd have..."

"What?" She was cross with him for trying to wriggle out of it. "Left me alone?"

"No. I'd have waited a while before hitting on you like that. I'm normally a better judge of a situation, believe me."

"You do this kind of thing regularly?" She wiped her face clean with her sleeve.

"As much as I can get away with. Call it a perk of the job. I'm on the road a lot. A man gets lonely."

"Even a man as handsome as you?"

"Especially." He stood up and went to the door. "Mind if we start again?"

Molly laughed. It was nice to be fooling around. "Go for it."

He walked across to the table. "Quiet tonight, isn't it?"

"It was busy when I came in. Full of locals. I guess I must have scared them all away." She raised her hands and curled her fingers into talons. Hissed like a snake and exposed her teeth. "I haven't the faintest idea what I might have done to make such an impression."

O'Malley rested his hand on her shoulder. "Then I suppose it's down to me to buy you a drink. What are you having?"

The Shallows

She ordered the same. He went and did the business. The only thing that was different this time was the flavour of the crisps.

*

O'Malley had her pinned to the door. He nibbled at her neck like a hungry beast. His bites were gentle and sent waves of pleasure through Molly's body.

His fingers slid under her top and stroked her breasts through the material of her bra. Her nipples hardened at the touch. The pleasure almost hurt. She wanted him to pinch them hard to break the pressure of the building pain so that he could start all over again. Her breathing was quick and her heart thumped like the fists of a champion.

God he was good. Even though he was paying her for the experience he was proud enough to give it his best shot.

Molly was going to suck out all the pleasure she could from it. The sex first, the spending of the money later.

There was no point brooding over Brad. Sure, she loved him. But he was gone. It was time for her to stand on her own two feet. She would do that as soon as her thighs stopped shaking and her pelvis stopped rocking to the rhythm of O'Malley's well-practised tune.

thirty

After a sit down meet with The Poet in *Make Do And Mend*, Brad felt good that one of his major problems was sorted. The false ID was on order for him and his family. A couple of days and the work would be done.

There was one more job to do in Newcastle and he could return to the hotel.

He walked up to Number Thirteen, Churchill Street for the fifth time. Stared at the bell the way he had on the first four occasions, stretched out a finger and pressed the plastic button before he could change his mind again. The chimes ran out like church bells. They were way too loud for a house of its size, a Victorian end-of-terrace built in the days when factories ruled the world.

His instincts told him to run, but his feet remained rooted to the ground. A scrabbling noise from inside told him that it was already too late. A key turned. The door opened as far as the security chain allowed. Half a face appeared in the gap. "What you want?"

"Mr Richardson? I'm Lieutenant Heap. Royal Navy. Blue Watch."

"I said what'd you want?" A whiff of alcohol came through on the man's breath.

"To help you find closure."

"Only closure round here happens to local business."

"Who is it David?" A woman's voice from a back room.

"Someone who knew our Kevin."

"Well, let them in for God's sake. The kids'll be nicking his trainers and his phone if you leave him out there any longer."

"I'll get the chain." The door closed and reopened. "Come in lad. The missus'd like a word."

"Thanks." Brad entered. Slipped his feet out of his shoes and put them to one side.

"They've got you well trained I see." Mrs Richardson.

"You should see me on parade."

"March yourself right on into the sitting room. We can talk better in there."

They all sat down on leather seats, the couple on the sofa and Brad on the chair. Along the wall, photographs of Kevin Richardson. School sports. The passing out parade. Saluting the Union flag. At a party with his arms around a woman and dancing very close. Seeing him like that, so full of life, gave Brad the shivers.

"You work the subs out of Faslane?" Kevin's dad, a hefty man with huge hands.

"Yes. Or at least, I did."

"Good on you son. Far as I'm concerned you're all heroes, the lot of you."

"You're in the minority, I reckon."

"Aye, well. There's not many would spend their lives living under the sea for ninety days at a stretch to protect their country."

"You don't have to make it sound so much like a prison sentence, David." Mrs Richardson rubbed her thumb into her palm. "You were with Kevin, you say. Tell me how he was."

"It's like Mr Richardson says. It's not an easy life. Being confined in a tube for three months can do funny things to you. You start to go nuts. The voyages were any longer, I think everyone would crack."

"We understand." Mr Richardson looked over at the photographs. Seemed to get lost in them for a moment and shook himself back to attention. "Kevin used to tell us. Not to worry, he'd say. The captain knew when to lighten the mood."

"They've got lots of tricks. When you reach breaking point, they throw something your way. A pizza or a box of things from home. The little things become important down there."

"Except it didn't work for our Kev this time."

There was silence. Brad didn't know how to continue. Sat there waiting for one of the others to speak.

"It was a lovely funeral." Mrs Richardson cracked first. "They had all the trimmings. The navy paid for everything. Buffet included."

"I'm sorry I couldn't be there." Truth be told, he hadn't wanted to be.

"I understand." Her eyes glazed over. The woman was lost.

"You've come to tell us about the end. Let's hear it."

Where to start? "Like I said before, it's not an easy life. Being crammed together like that. No personal space. Relatives and friends so far away. It plays on your mind."

"It must have messed up Kevin something proper."

"I was there to listen to him. Like a counsellor or a priest. To see if I could help."

"Fat lot of good you did, then."

The old bastard was right. Brad deserved it. "He was in a state. Things weren't going well. He was missing home. You guys and Julie."

"That's her up there." Mrs Richardson pointed over to the picture. "At their engagement party."

"She's beautiful." Even though she wasn't. "How is she taking it?"

"No idea." Kevin's Dad. We don't hear from her."

"She needs to move on." Mrs Richardson picked at her skirt. "A lovely girl like that has a whole life ahead of her. We didn't want to hold her back."

"Of course." Brad wondered how he would cope if Molly set off in a new direction. Decided he'd break as easily as the china ornaments on the mantelpiece if they hit the hearth.

"I don't care what she's up to. I want to know about this bleeding heart of his."

It was more difficult than Brad imagined it would be. In his rehearsals, he just told it straight. Now there were two pairs of eyes fixed upon him, he wanted to back-track. He ran through his lines again and began. "We can all get lonely in the sub. And there are no women down there. Sometimes a man has to turn to someone to find some comfort."

Mr Richardson stood up. "If you're about to say what I think you are, I'd rather we stopped right now."

"Leave him alone, David. I want to know the truth. We can't go through the rest of our lives with our heads surrounded by mist."

"We bloody well can."

"It just happens to some of the lads when we're at sea. It doesn't mean anything. They're just letting off steam."

"How'd you mean?" Her voice shook.

"I'm just saying that for some of the men it's part of the life."

"You're lying." Mr Richardson's fists clenched. "He wasn't like that. I know he wasn't."

"I agree. Only there are strong characters on board any ship. They pick on the vulnerable. They find weakness the way sharks smell blood."

Mr Richardson put his fingers in his ears. "Shut up. Get out of my house and take your filthy mind with you."

His wife stood. Took hold of his arms and pulled at them. "We need to find out, David. You know we do." He shook her off. Stomped across the room and grabbed Brad's jacket at each shoulder.

"I told you, we don't want your frigging lies."

Brad was hauled from the chair. His feet left the ground.

"Don't do this, David. Put him down."

"The hell I will."

Brad floated into the hallway. Flew through the front door. Landed on his head on the pavement. Wondered why some people found it so difficult to accept the facts of life.

thirty one

Worst part of the job was the paperwork. Shanks was half way through filling out a report on a brawl between the navy and the natives in the centre of town. The phone rang. He hoped it might offer him a lifeline. A few hours out of the office. Something hands on. He lifted the receiver.

"Ah, Captain Shanks. Glad I caught you." The voice was posh. Male. Pompous. It could be anyone of a higher rank. "Briggs here. I've got some news. I'm afraid it's not of the good kind."

When the commander called it rarely ended well. "What have you got, sir?"

"It's Heap. Turns out he's not sleeping with the fishes after all."

"Sir?"

"He's alive and well and stirring the pot again. It seems he can't let it lie. We had a call from a Mr Richardson."

"I see." Shanks dug his thumb into his neck muscles. Gave the knots a rub.

"He's not a happy bunny. Heap went round. Threw all sorts of smut at the parents and expected them to be grateful for the information."

Shanks knew that was merely a question of perspective. He pictured the scene in a different way. There was something noble in what Heap had done. Visiting victims was a hell of a job. His actions deserved respect even if his manner was off the mark.

"How did they take it?"

"Mr Richardson claims he threw him out on his arse. Can't say I blame the man."

Shanks picked up his pen. Located his notebook and got ready to make notes. "And this was when?"

"This afternoon. At the family home."

"Which means he can't have got far."

"You'll alert the police in the area as soon as we're done. After that I want you down there making a personal visit to the house. Apologise. Offer them something. Anything within reason."

"Sir."

"Send me written reports every two hours."

"Understood." Shanks drew a circle on his pad. Sketched in some eyes, a nose, a mouth and a Hitler moustache.

"We need to catch this bastard before he does any more damage. Who knows what he's capable of?"

"We'll get him." As he said the words he realised that something didn't feel right. He didn't believe they were about to catch him. He wasn't certain he even wanted to.

"Make sure that net closes tight. The sooner you end this, the better."

"Don't you worry about a thing."

"I shan't. After all, it's not my neck on the line here. It's yours."

Shanks stabbed his pen into the middle of his doodle's eye. Went right through to the next page. Ruined the ballpoint and tossed it into the bin. Waited for the commander to sign off and got to work.

thirty two

The restaurant had long since finished serving food but the bar was still open. There was enough of a crowd to give a healthy buzz to the place.

Brad was surprised there were so many people out this early in the week. He was pleased to have their company. Not that he wanted conversation. He just didn't feel like being alone.

His newspaper lay on the table, a picture of Molly looking up at him. She wasn't on page one anymore and the photo was small. Maybe the world would forget about her soon. He traced around her face with his finger. Stroked her mouth and sighed.

A hand patted his shoulder. It was far too soft a touch to be the police. He didn't bother to turn round and see who it was.

"Been in the wars then?" The lady from reception.

She stepped into view. Took a seat at the table without asking. She looked different. More human. That might have had something to do with the glass of wine she was holding. Her dress was tight and low-cut and she'd dispensed with the spectacles. The look suited her.

"I was in Newcastle on business. Wasn't looking where I was going and tripped over a kerb."

"And landed on your face. You poor sausage." Her words were wet with the slur of booze. She reached over and stroked his cheek. He pulled his head away and sat back in his chair.

"It looks worse than it feels."

"I'm glad to hear it." She turned to the barman. Her movements were clumsy and she almost lost her balance. "Another one for the gentleman and more wine for me please Sid."

"Not for me. I'm tired. I need..."

"Nonsense." She nodded over to Sid and he snapped into action. "You can never refuse a drink on the house. It's just not done."

The Shallows

It was true. And Brad had never turned down a free pint in his life. "Thanks. I appreciate it."

"Iris." She slid back in her chair until she was practically lying down. "Since you didn't ask. The name's Iris." She held out her arm, her hand limp like a princess expecting to be kissed.

"Brad." He took her fingers. Gave them a squeeze. It was all she was going to get. He looked around to see if anyone was watching. Everyone was too engrossed in their own chatter to notice anything.

Iris finished the wine in her glass. Sat up and put the empty on the table.

"I know. Now tell me a story Brad. I like to listen to stories before I go to bed."

"I'm all out of them just now."

"Well, perhaps the next drink will liberate them from your mind."

The barman appeared. Put down a pint of cider and a flute of something fizzy.

Iris touched Sid on the arm. Left her hand there. "Thank you darling. And have one yourself."

"Cheers." The man limped back to the bar. Opened the till, took out a couple of quid and dropped it into the pot of tips.

"You're a very generous woman."

"Oh, you don't know the half of it." She smiled and sipped at her drink. "You can ask anyone around here. They'll tell you exactly what a giving person I am." Her hand found Brad's knee.

His insides scrunched up into a ball. He kept his leg still, sat back and created some distance. Took a good swallow of cider and waited for her next move.

"I'm addicted to the fizz." Iris moved towards him. "They call me the magpie, you know. Anything that shines I have to have."

"Oh?"

"And your eyes are just full of sparkle." Her laugh was practically a purr. She shifted her hand further up Brad's leg. He looked over the bar. The waiter did his best to pretend he wasn't watching and dropped his gaze.

Brad's cheeks warmed underneath his beard.

Iris's hand moved further towards his crotch. He pressed his thighs together to stop her getting all the way.

She giggled when he did that. Narrowed her eyes. "Come on, Brad. You can't let the bridal suite go to waste." She leaned close. Whispered. "The only thing a four-poster is good for is for shagging. Truth is, that pretty much goes for me, too." Her hot breath tickled his ear.

Brad's stomach tingled. He looked down at the table and saw the picture of Molly staring at them both.

Iris's tongue licked his lobe.

Things had gone far enough. He stood up as quickly as he would if an officer entered the room. Cider spilled from his glass. Iris lunged forwards. Made a grab for his waist and fell to the floor.

Holy crap. Every customer in the place was looking over.

Iris was on her knees, a pool of champagne spreading on the wooden floorboards beneath her.

Brad put his pint town. He held out his hands to let everyone know he was innocent. "Sorry," he said. He turned to the waiter. "I think your boss has had a little too much of a good time for one night."

Iris reached up. Grabbed hold of his shirt and tried to pull him down. Brad took her wrist and tugged the fabric from her grip. He stepped backwards, brushed himself down and then jogged towards the stairs.

Last thing her heard from the bar was Iris laughing. She sounded so free and happy. Just like the little dog in the nursery rhyme.

thirty three

Eleven o'clock at night. Molly had been waiting since nine. The pain of missing Brad had taken over her body. Not even the bottle of wine had eased her suffering.

The only antidote she'd found so far was sex. Her time with Tony O'Malley had been pure joy. He took her to a different dimension. It's what she needed right now. A distraction. A visit to a different time. A place where nobody else existed and history was nothing more than a seven-letter word.

Her romp had been a profitable excursion to boot. She found two-hundred quid on her pile of clothes when she got up and dressed. It was the best paid job she'd ever had.

Another payday like that would buy her more time.

So where the hell was he? He told her he'd be there as soon as he finished work. That he'd treat her to dinner and show her how the Irish treated a lady.

The door to the hotel slammed open. Laughter filled the air. The barman put his crossword down and got ready for action.

Into the bar careered Tony O'Malley and a woman in a pinstriped suit. They were clinging onto each other for support. They scuttled to the bar like a crab over sand.

"Two pints of your finest ale." O'Malley's voice was loud and condescending. There was nothing of the suave sophistication of the night before. "And one for yourself my good man."

The woman reached up and threw her arms round O'Malley's neck. She lifted herself onto her tiptoes. Their lips met and they spent time sucking the faces off each other. O'Malley's hands dropped to grab her buttocks. She grabbed his tie and pulled it down to half-mast. It was revolting.

The barman put the drinks on the table and gave a diplomatic cough.

O'Malley waved him away. "On second thoughts, we'll not be needing any more refreshment. I think we've got business of an important financial variety to attend to up in the room." He swayed as he spoke. Almost fell. The woman in the suit held him up. When he was steady, they walked to the door as if nothing had happened.

He caught sight of Molly just before he left. Stopped and put his hand to the side of his mouth. "You were great darling." It was supposed to be a whisper. He might as well have been calling to the house next door. "And thanks. But it's always better when it's free."

What a prick. Molly wanted to throw her drink into his face. Instead she froze. Her whole body was stuck

The woman tugged O'Malley's arm and they disappeared into the foyer.

Molly thought of a thousand things she could shout after him. A million ways she might inflict pain. Remembered there were still bullets left in the gun in the car. Decided the man wasn't worth the price of the lead.

thirty four

Three days under wraps. Hiding in the hotel room and only going out for essentials. It was driving Molly nuts. Shem was a good lad, but he couldn't cope with being laid up all the time. He practically broke the bed before they left, bouncing up and down on it like it was a new line in trampolines. She almost literally had to peel him off the ceiling to get him out to the car.

There was no way she could have him sitting still all day, pestering her with questions and stories for the entire journey.

The boy needed to let off some steam. They drove to the swimming pool and paid for a session.

It was a fantastic morning. They had waves and fountains, floats to play on and the flume at the side of the pool was just the ticket.

As she blow-dried her hair and looked in the mirror, she noticed that the chlorine in the water had taken away some of the dye. If she bleached it, it would make her more difficult to spot. It wouldn't do anything for the bedraggled look though. The only way to sort that would be to get a professional hairdresser on the job. With the budget dipping under two-hundred pounds, that wasn't going to be possible.

She dressed and collected Shem from the shower. She wrapped him in his towel, patted him dry then let him sort himself out. She went off and bought a coffee from the machine.

Shem came out into the cafe with his trousers on inside out. Molly admired his good looks and skinny frame.

There was another family at the table next to theirs. They were squabbling. A mother and father who didn't mind scrapping in front of their kid.

Molly did her best to ignore them. She took Shem over to the machine and punched in the numbers for a hot chocolate and a couple of packs of crisps.

When they got back to their seats, the other family had disappeared, leaving all their things on and around the table.

On the floor was an open handbag with a stuffed wallet poking out of the top. It was asking to be stolen.

Molly sipped at her coffee. It was boiling hot and burned her mouth. It was what she needed to ground herself. There was no way she could risk taking someone's cash. If they caught her, they'd take Shem away. For the sake of a couple of quid it really wasn't worth it.

Shem reached out for his drink. "Eat your crisps first," Molly told him. "Give the chocolate time to cool down."

She watched her son follow her instructions. Saw him notice the wallet and look back at her. His expression was difficult to read. She guessed he was telling her not to do anything rash. Couldn't blame him for that. She'd put him through plenty these past couple of days.

The temptation just became stronger. The urge grew so large within her that she had to leave. "I need to pee." Molly got up. "Don't drink that till I get back."

Shem nodded and she left him to it.

From the toilet cubicle she heard the family arguing in one of the changing rooms.

"I can't afford another pair of goggles for God's sake. Do you think they grow on trees lad?" A man's voice with a Geordie lilt.

"Leave him alone RJ. He didn't mean to leave them, did you son?"

Instead of answering, the boy burst into tears.

"See what you've done now. You've gone and upset him."

"You're worried about the bairn? What about the money we're pissing down the drain bringing him up. Least he could do would be to look after the things we buy him. It's the third sodding pair this year."

"Don't worry Will. Your father doesn't mean it. We'll go to the desk and see if anyone's handed them in."

There was a lot of banging and under-the-breath swearing.

Molly flushed the toilet. Washed her hands. Walked out and saw the family grab their things and storm off in silence. She was disappointed that the opportunity to take the cash was gone. Relieved that the temptation had disappeared.

She joined her son who had done what he was asked and finally got to drink his chocolate.

Soon as he finished, they left.

The family mustn't have found their goggles. They were marching back in, the child being dragged by the arm like a prisoner.

"Come on Mum." Shem took Molly's hand and pulled her in the direction of their car. "We need to get going."

It was a fair point. If they went for it, they could be half way to Grange before stopping for lunch.

They packed their swimming gear into the boot and got into their seats. Molly pulled out of the parking space and drove up to the roundabout. In the rear view she saw the family at the entrance. They were still fighting, only this time it was more intense. Looked like they might even come to blows.

Molly turned onto the main road and switched the radio on.

As she joined the A1, Shem hit the mute button on the stereo.

"When you shot that man at the farm, you were doing a bad thing for a good reason, right?"

Molly didn't know how to answer. Didn't feel like going through the endless tunnels of whys and hows that he sometimes drilled. "I did it to make sure you and your daddy were safe."

"That's what I mean." He lifted his glasses and rubbed his nose. "You did well. Dad said."

Her face flushed. Listening to her son talk about murder in this way was just wrong. It definitely wasn't in any of the good parenting books she'd read.

Shem fidgeted in his seat. A morning swim and he still had energy to burn. He pulled up his swimming bag and pulled something from it.

Molly took her eyes from the road and looked down. In his hands was the wallet she wanted to steal at the pool.

"I know it's a bad thing I did, but it's okay. God knows I did it for a good reason. We need the money more than they do." He was right on that score. "So I took it when you were in the bathroom. You're not cross are you Mum?"

Molly took a hand from the wheel and ruffled his hair. "Course I'm not." She bit her lip hard. Needed to keep a straight face for her son's sake.

"Then let's go to find Daddy." He turned the music up again. The Beachboys.

The harmonies diluted all of Molly's cares. She smiled down at her son. "How much did we get then, Shem?" Maybe she could make an appointment with a hairdresser after all.

thirty five

The Poet was a genius. Brad's ID was nigh on perfect. A complete set of documents to suit every occasion. The work on Molly and Shem's passports were just as good. Thirty grand seemed cheap for the quality and the short time it had taken to get it together.

With it all locked in a suitcase and chained to the passenger seat, Brad felt secure. He set off in the direction of Grange, grateful that he'd never have to see that ridiculous woman in Berwick ever again.

The drive was exactly what he needed to plan his next move. Staying in the country was out of the question, whether he hooked up with Molly again or not. The Navy wouldn't give up the chase, nor would the police. As for Red Fenton, if he ever got a sniff of Brad he would end up as fishing bait.

Best option would be to get hold of a boat. Put all of his sailing skills into operation. He was built for the sea and there were plenty of gypsies out there proving it could be done. He had enough money left to buy something serious with room for his wife and Shem to live without suffocating each other. There would still be enough left over to keep them going for a good couple of years.

Instead of heading straight for Grange, he made a detour to Whitehaven to check out the marina.

He parked up at a fancy looking restaurant and decided he was hungry enough to eat.

The weather was pleasant and he sat outside. Ordered the mussels and a beer and devoured the lot in minutes. A sticky toffee pudding and another drink later, he was ready to face the world. He took a fifty from his jacket, left it on the table and wandered down to the harbour.

As he mooched around the marina, he let his imagination loose. He pictured the family moored up off some Greek island. Shem jumping into the Med. Molly stretched out under a parasol on the deck. A bottle of chilled Retsina with a bowl of olives on the table. The radio on. The sun warming the skin. It was his idea of paradise.

Each boat he passed suggested possibilities, even the twenty-footers.

At the end of the walkway, a sign caught his attention. FOR SALE. NO TIME WASTERS.

It had to be worth a look.

He kept going and reached a fine looking Colvic Victor 40 ketch. Deck saloon. Two helm positions. Ropes clean and neatly coiled. Sails in good order. On the old side, but well looked after. The name BETSY was painted on the prow.

A middle-aged man wearing shorts and a rich tan sat on board and drank coffee.

"Can't you read?" The voice was American. Less than friendly. The guy wasn't going to get many offers with an attitude like that.

"Perfectly."

The man stood. Walked over to the stern.

"I'm not interested in giving free rides. You want out to sea there are plenty of charters. Go take your pick." He turned his back on Brad and returned to the coffee.

"Why don't you tell me how much you're asking? That way we can both work out whether we're wasting our time or not."

The skipper laughed. "She may be long in the tooth, but she ain't going for a song. Forty-nine thousand five hundred's what I'm after. I won't be dipping under that for no one."

"How about I come down and you can tell me why you're asking so much for this old bird?"

The man scratched his head. Stood again. "I'll have your head spinning in no time."

Brad stepped onto *Betsy*. The American held out his hand. "The name's Duke." Could be because he had the square jaw of John Wayne.

They shook. "Rudy." The name on Brad's passport. It was like trying on a new uniform, stiff and unfamiliar. At least it was easy to remember. "So give me the tour and let me know what I've been missing."

It was an impressive layout. Nine berths in all. Two of those were in the fore peak. The double cabins were a fair size. The saloon had a microwave and a television as well as the usual fittings. Brad's family would have enough space to stay out of each other's pockets. It was perfect.

All he needed to know now was her sea worthiness. "She been anywhere?"

Duke's laugh had the growl of a Rottweiler about it. "I brought her over from the States. Been back there twice. Took it in her stride every time."

"Then why're you selling?"

There was no laugh this time. "Cancer."

"I'm sorry."

"Me too. My wife's not doing so good. I want her to have the best she can get. Luxuries like this don't seem to mean the same when she's not here to share them with."

Brad understood. He thought of how it would feel to leave without Molly. Blocked out the sadness as soon as it rose inside. Wasn't ready to give up hope. "That must be tough."

"Decisions like that are easier than you think. When you get to my age, there's no time for fooling around." He walked up the steps and back up top. "I've been saving the best till last."

They went over to the engine house and Duke lifted the lid. "That's a Thorneycroft 155." Not that Brad needed telling. "Only a couple of years old. Barely a hundred hours on the clock."

It was a sweet looking thing.

"Let me hear her go."

Duke entered the wheelhouse. Fired her up.

The rhythm was pure. The exhaust clean. The noise low.

"She purrs, don't she?" Duke looked down on the works like a proud father.

"She does that." Last thing on the checklist, a trip out to sea. "How about you take me out for an hour or so. Let me get a feel for her."

"I told you before, you want to play sailor there's plenty of charter boats available."

Brad took a bundle of cash from his pocket. "I can pay you. If I end up buying, you can take it off the price. I don't, you just made yourself a quick grand."

Duke rubbed his chin. Nodded. Took the money. "Give me five minutes."

Five minutes Brad could spare. A tune popped into his head. *Can't Buy Me Love*. Lennon was right about that, but should have known more than anyone how much easier life was when there was money in your pocket.

thirty six

The hotel lounge at the Northwood was as grand as they come. It hadn't changed a bit since their honeymoon. The only thing that was missing was Brad.

Molly's heart pounded every time she heard a car come up the gravel path. No matter how unlikely it seemed that Brad would turn up, she couldn't stifle her hope.

Shem was sure they'd be reunited. He'd talked of nothing else since Kendal. He sat upright, peering out of the window like a young meerkat.

The waitress brought over their order on a tray. Popped a pot of tea, an apple juice and an enormous slice of carrot cake onto the table. Left them to enjoy their treat.

"You think he'll be here soon?" Shem picked up his serviette and took out the spoon and fork. Offered them to his mother. She took the fork.

"If we're lucky." She cut into the cake. Made sure she got a decent amount of the frosting. Popped it into her mouth and let the flavours melt into her tongue. "Mmmmm." The gentle spice, moist sponge and the crunch of the walnuts mingled with the sugary lemon of the icing. It wasn't better than sex, but it came close.

Shem took his turn. His eyes popped wide open in delight. For the moment, at least, it appeared that he'd forgotten about seeing his father again.

A cake this good deserved to be savoured. Instead, it was demolished.

Molly checked her new style in the reflection of the silver sugar bowl. Preened herself and sorted out a few stray hairs. The hairdresser had done a fine job. Brought some respectability back. It was exactly what she needed to be allowed into a place like this.

Shem licked the crumbs from the corner of his mouth. "Can we stay here for the night?"

Bless him. "I don't have the money." They couldn't even afford the Travelodge. A few nights in the car was what they had to look forward to. She didn't have the heart to tell him yet.

"We've got the wallet."

"It's too expensive." She brushed his cheek with her fingers. "If we need to come here for tea every day, we have to save as much as possible."

"But Daddy said he would come."

"He'll be here if he can sweetheart."

"You should ask the man at the desk. See if he has a room."

"They're not allowed to give out private information."

"It's not private. He's our dad."

"But they don't know that."

"I'll tell them." Shem got up and marched out of the lounge. Must have been the sugar making him crazy. He was at reception before she could stop him. "Is my dad staying here?"

The young man smiled. "Is he supposed to be?"

"If his work went well."

"Does he have a name?" The clerk was gentle and had a kind face.

"Brad."

Molly picked up her pace. Had to get there before Shem blew the whole thing.

"Brad who?"

"Collins." Molly got there just in time to intercept. "Brad Collins."

"And you are?"

"Mrs Collins."

"Then let me have a look." The man clicked his mouse on the computer below the desktop. Molly noticed something odd about his hands as he scrolled through the pages. She counted the thumb and fingers and only reached four. His pinkie was missing. "Sorry. Your husband's not here. When were you expecting him?"

"Some time today. I'll check my messages." She tried to avoid looking at the hand but her eyes were drawn there anyway. The scar looked raw and mean.

"If you wait in the lounge and he comes while I'm on shift, I'll let him know."

"That's very kind. We'll do that." Molly grabbed Shem's arm. Took him back to their table. Pushed him into his chair. "Drink your juice. Pretend that didn't happen."

Shem looked bemused.

"We can't tell anyone about who we are. It's got to be our secret. If they find out, we'll all be in big trouble."

Shem's face tightened. His breathing halted. It was the way he behaved when he was trying to hide his hurt.

Molly picked him up. Lifted him onto her knee. Cuddled him close and let his feelings pour out into the ether.

thirty seven

It was dark when Brad arrived in Grange-Over-Sands.

The trip on *Betsy* took longer than planned. She was a honey. The perfect home for his family. He shook hands with Duke at the asking price and worked out the formalities. As long as it all went to plan, she'd be his this time tomorrow.

He should have been happy to be back here, but the hotel screwed with his mind. For every memory his surroundings triggered there was an enormous kick from reality. Each high brought a deeper low. He was being pulled apart by Yin and Yang.

In the bar he remembered the way Molly looked, her eyes sparkling more than her champagne. The restaurant reminded him of haggis lasagne. In the grounds he located the tree where they kissed under the stars.

In his room he replayed the sex over and over like film on a loop. He would never get to sleep. His conscience wouldn't let him. He needed to find his family. They had to be here in town somewhere and he wouldn't rest until he found them.

thirty eight

Two hours of shagging had crippled John Locke. Doreen wasn't like any other woman he'd ever known. She just couldn't get enough. It should have been a dream come true only it had more in common with being stuck in a nightmare.

All his attempts at showing off were playing hell with his sciatica. He was bending into positions his physiotherapist wouldn't believe.

When his manhood was spent, he used his fingers and his tongue to satisfy Doreen's hunger. Just when he thought it was safe for him to get some sleep, she perked up and took out her favourite toys. He'd done things in the past few days than he could never have imagined.

Sod's law that as soon as she fell asleep Locke was wide awake.

He threw on her dressing gown and went downstairs to the lounge. There was coffee in the pot and he had everything he needed in his case.

He spread his notes around on the dining room table and unfolded a map on the floor.

The whole mess had started in the north. Their next stop was Eyemouth where they stayed in a caravan owned by Molly's aunt.

Brad had disappeared after a trip out with Red. He popped up in Newcastle after that, at the Richardson home.

Molly wasn't quite so straightforward. She pulled the trigger at the dope plantation and held up a newsagent for a measly couple-of-hundred quid. After that, she was seen in Alnwick.

Stealing the wallet was a lucky break for the police. The CCTV had picked out their car and identified the registration plate. It would simply be a matter of time before they were spotted by a human or a machine and then they would hammer the nail in the coffin. Unless Molly switched rides along the way.

Put it all together and there could be little doubt that the family were drifting south. Locke figured they would be gravitating to the same point.

The grandmother's cottage in Cornwall was his best bet. The Cornish force had been informed. If he was lucky, Locke reckoned he might even get a trip down there.

He took out his ruler and a pencil and set to try to work out some kind of time frame.

"John." Doreen's dulcet tones. "Are you awake?"

Her foot appeared at the top of the stairs. It was followed by a leg, then the rest of her. She was dressed in a black negligee that would have been better used as net curtains.

"Oh John." She put on the voice of a movie star. "I can think of a few things you could do with that equipment. Bring it up and I'll show you what I have in mind."

His frame wilted. He folded up his map, gathered up his tools and trudged up to get another dose of education in the ways of sex and depravity.

thirty nine

Parking in Grange was a nightmare. Molly drove round a couple of times before she saw a car pulling out of a space.

She grabbed the spot and checked the sign. Waiting limited to two hours. That would be plenty of time. They crossed the road to the railway station to take advantage of the toilets.

A splash of cold water brought Molly back to life. Washed away some of her tiredness. Their night in the Volvo had been straightforward enough, but she wouldn't be able to do it too many times before needing a bed to sleep in.

They cut through the park and stopped to feed the ducks with the remains of their breakfast. Unusual birds with bright markings came over to chomp on the croissant crumbs and the remains of a sausage roll. They were beautiful creatures, uninhibited by thoughts and feelings and financial woes. In the next life, she wanted to be a mallard.

They wandered through a car park and up the concrete ramp onto the promenade.

It was difficult to imagine the dangers lurking out on the bay when it looked so tranquil. The place was notorious for the swift-changing tides and the quicksand. Many had been caught out over the years and even today the only way to cross was by guide. The view stretched into the distance, miles of marsh grass and sand and sea, the hills on the other side of the estuary looking like a watercolour painting. The air was still and warm. It was as though the world was giving her a transfusion. Allowing her to forget her troubles for a while. A break from her sadness and stress.

"Look Mum, crazy golf." They were suckers for it. Couldn't pass a course without giving it a go. It was a family tradition and they weren't about to change that now.

"Just what we need. Winner gets an ice cream." They found the Youth Project hut where they kept the equipment. Were talked into a day ticket allowing them to play all the sports on offer for as long as they wanted. Bowls, table tennis, basketball and pitch and putt were theirs for a fiver.

They took their gear and headed over for the first tee on the course, a windmill with three tunnels to choose from. Shem lined up the ball, gave it a tap and watched it go. It went through the middle tube, bounced against the bricks at the back and rebounded into the hole.

His victory dance was a joy to behold. The spins and whoops were those of a little boy. It was good to see that she hadn't damaged him too much with everything she had put him through.

From then on the whole experience was a treat. Every shot was absorbing. Each challenge engrossing. It was such a lot of fun that they totally forgot to keep a note of the time.

forty

Brad's feet hurt from all his walking. Grange was deceptively big. What he needed to do was buy a bicycle. Later on he would check out the ads in the local shops. See if he couldn't find something that was his size.

His stomach rumbled. Told him it was lunch time.

He knew where he wanted to eat. The bakery cafe where he and Molly once shared cheesecake while they sheltered from the rain. It was a cosy memory. The storm hadn't passed by the time they were done, so they ran back to the hotel and got soaked. Jumped straight into the bath to warm up. Ended up making love in mountains of foam and smelling like bars of soap for the rest of the day.

As far as he could remember, the cafe was down by the station. He wandered down the hill, already salivating.

The sign for the bakery was exactly where he thought it would be. He picked up the pace and then stopped in his tracks.

In the bay, a parking attendant was checking out a vehicle. It was a familiar looking Volvo, a whole heap of bags and junk piled up in the boot of the estate. Under a layer of dust he read the plate. Knew immediately it was Molly and Shem's.

His body went weak for a moment. It was as though his spine had melted. He rested his hands upon his knees to prevent himself from falling. Slowed his breath. Counted down from ten to one. Pushed himself upright and looked over at the warden who was preparing to write out a ticket. Brad's instincts took over and he walked into the gap between the man and the car.

"You've got a problem with this vehicle?" Maybe he could stall things. Persuade the guy to turn a blind eye. Do another round of the town and check back later.

"Is it yours?"

"No. I just wondered if you might cut these guys a break. They're clearly on holiday." He pointed through the glass. "Look at all their gear."

The man scratched his nose with the end of his stylus. "Not my problem, sir."

"But you don't want people leaving the town with a bad taste in their mouths."

"To be honest, the fewer tourists come back the easier my job becomes." He typed the details into his device. Waited for a moment for it to process.

"Why not give them five minutes, eh?"

The warden pointed at the screen. "Not this time, mate." He fished a mobile phone from his jacket. "The police have an APB out for this one." He turned his back on Brad and made the call.

Brad set off to the bakery, his head swimming in a sea of panic. At the door he turned back to the car. Stared at the sleeping bag unrolled in the back. The mess of chocolate bar wrappers and empty crisp packets. Looked down to see Shem's teddy bear sitting on the passenger seat waiting for its owner to return.

His body froze. This was the place he needed to be. The only spot in town he knew for certain his family would show up. It was also the most dangerous place on earth for him just now. The warden had already called. The police would be there in minutes. If he were to stand any chance of staying free, he would have to get away.

He crossed the road. Ran into the park. Admired the ducks on the lake and made a bee line for the hotel.

forty one

Molly stopped at the kerb and caught her breath while she waited for Shem. He ran up the hill, his jacket tied around his waist and his cheeks red and hot. If Brad had been there, he'd have picked him up. Carried him along for the rest of the way and saved the day.

"That's it." Shem reached the pavement. He bent over and rested his hands on his knees. She messed his hair. "Nearly there."

"Okay Mum." He straightened himself. Held her hand. Looked up at her and smiled. The corners of the lenses of his spectacles were misted up with sweat. She'd buy him an ice cream when this was done and let him cool down before they did anything else.

They jogged down the hill and stopped at the crossing, but didn't bother to press the button. The traffic was backed up all the way, none of it moving.

Flashing lights caught Molly's attention. She looked in their direction. Saw two police cars double-parked alongside her Volvo. Stepped to the other side of the road and pulled Shem's arm back like she was applying a brake. Her heart went into overdrive as she surveyed the scene.

Most of the action took place around her car. The officers peered in and tried the doors. A warden waved his arms and stopped the vehicles heading into town. A group of tourists gathered to have a nosey and a gang of walkers ignored the whole thing.

Molly's lip trembled.

They had the Volvo. All their possessions. Everything they had apart from her handbag, her purse and the clothes that they stood in. Her husband was dead and her lungs hurt. What chance did they have? How could she allow her son to endure a life on the run with none of the trappings? Steal all of his opportunities because she wanted to stay free.

The realisation hit her. If she surrendered, she'd get a bed for the night. Food and clean clothes. Shem would be sent to live with her sister and his cousins. Grow up in a house with love and school and something to look forward to.

It was all over.

She set off walking. Casual, as if she were just going for a stroll. Comfortable with her decision to turn herself in.

Shem tugged at her hand. She dragged him along down towards the action.

"Stop!" He pulled hard. Brought her to a halt.

"It's the only way, Shem. I need to give up." Tears poured down her cheeks. She didn't bother to hide them.

"No, Mum." He let go of her arm and took a step back. "We're not giving up. Not until we've found Dad."

The determination on his face told her everything. This time no meant no.

forty two

Duke stood on the deck of Betsy and took the last drag from a fat cigar. "Simple pleasures." Smoke puffed out from his mouth as he spoke. He docked the stub out into an ashtray and walked back into the saloon. "I don't get to do that nearly enough these days. My other half doesn't allow me."

A bottle of champagne in a plastic bucket of ice dominated the table. Duke took it out, twisted the cork and pulled it free. The fizz bubbled up and erupted. Brad held two tumblers out to be filled.

"Here's to many years of happy sailing." Duke raised his glass. Brad did the same. They knocked it back.

The crisp flavour woke up Brad's taste buds. It was just the tonic he needed. "That's good stuff."

"The best they had on the shelves. Thanks to you, I can afford it." Duke went to pour again.

Brad put his hand in the way. "Not for me. I've got a lot to take care of." He wondered when he'd last refused a drop of champers. Couldn't recall. What he did know was that it would require a clear head to find his family and whip them away from under the noses of the police.

forty three

Doreen cooked Locke lunch and it appeared that he was the dessert. She was all ready to apply the squirty cream when his mobile rang.

"We've found the car in the Bonnie and Clyde case boss." Hawley rattled his words out like an excited kid.

"Whereabouts?" Doreen chewed on his nipple. There was nothing sexy about the pain.

"Grange-Over-Sands."

"How soon can you pick me up?" He ripped his flesh from Doreen's teeth and stood up.

"I'm already on my way."

Locke opened his wardrobe. Took out a shirt. Tried to hide his smile. He had never been so delighted to have a day off interrupted by a call from the station.

forty four

Molly's bones were sore. The cold had seeped through her flesh and was attacking her marrow. She lit the last of the cigarettes. All those years without a smoke and she had demolished a whole packet in one night. She despised herself for her weakness. Was reminded about her pathetic life with every breath. Could barely tolerate the tobacco stink of her clothes. Wanted to leap in the pool to clean herself off. More than that. Craved sinking to the bottom to revel in the silence there.

The disused lido was like the mausoleum of an Indian princess. Not even the graffiti and the crumbling stone masked the elegance of the space. How spectacular it must once have been.

She looked on the mirrored surface of the pool. Watched the reflected clouds skirt by in the gentle light of the dawn. Sucked on her Silk Cut and held the buzz in her lungs.

Shem stirred under the arches of the old diving boards. He was curled into a ball, sucking on his thumb.

It broke her heart to think she'd brought him to this. If things carried on, she would only make it all worse.

He looked over at her and smiled.

Molly hid her hand behind her back and flicked the cigarette away. She walked over to her son, wrapped her arms around him and cuddled him close.

*

It wasn't much of a plan. To sneak out of the building the way they'd entered. Go to the shops and buy the food they would need for a couple of days while it was still early. Maybe get hold of a blanket to share when the cold returned. Come back to their hideout and stay there until there was a chance the coast was clear. That was as far as it went.

Cornwall seemed a million miles away. Happiness utterly out of reach.

Her anxiety grew with every step along the promenade. It was getting so big she thought she might explode.

Shem's voice was a stream of noise. Sometimes she tuned in, others she lost him completely. It was as if there was a loose wire in her head. Her sight was blurred and she couldn't get the world to focus. She was exhausted and needed to stop. To switch herself off and shut out all her pain.

"Do you know what Shem?" She stopped at the playground next to the railway track. "It might be safer if I go alone. Can you stay here for a while and wait for me?"

"Course I can."

She knew his answer before he spoke. He loved the train that dominated the space. Made a great engine driver for his imaginary passengers. "I tell you what. Why don't I leave you some money to play with? So you can give change after you sell the tickets." She took her purse from her bag. Opened it and pulled out a ten-pound note. Had second thoughts. Passed him the whole purse. "Take care of it won't you. There's a lot of cash in there."

"Thanks Mum." The smile on his face was brighter than the sun. He turned and ran in the direction of the gate.

"Hey. Aren't you forgetting something?"

Shem stopped. Looked at her for a moment and then sprinted into her arms.

She squeezed him tight. Whispered into his ear. "I love you, Shem. I always will."

He kissed her cheek. Hugged her back. Let go and went off to make sure the train left the station on time.

Molly wiped her nose on her sleeve and walked away. She climbed down from the promenade onto the marsh and set off in the direction of the far shore.

The grass prickled the top of her legs. Her feet squelched in the soft sand. She picked up her pace. Kept her eyes on the horizon and hoped everything would be over very soon.

forty five

Brad cycled to the promenade, slowed to a halt and dismounted. He took his bike to the railings and chained it up.

The sun burned into his eyes. He screwed them shut and rubbed his face hoping to bring himself back to life. A night without sleep had taken its toll. A final circuit of the walkway was all he had the energy for. If he didn't find them, he would go to the hotel for breakfast and a nap.

His legs protested as he set off, stiffening as he put one foot in front of the other. His hands shook from the effort of his search. It was no good. He was done. The bench ahead was as far as he was going to get. He limped over and sat down.

He checked his watch. Half-past seven. It wouldn't be long before the police saturated the streets. Brad would have to skulk indoors until the evening came, like a vampire hiding from the light.

Overhead a flock of gulls flew out across the bay. Brad wished he could sprout wings. That he could coast along in the air-currents above the town and find his wife and child.

He looked out over the sands. Watched a train cross the bridge over the water. Turned to his right and was surprised to see the dark shape of a human figure plodding through the muddy sand. He hoped they knew what they were doing. It was treacherous territory to wander in.

Whoever it was, they were barely moving. Brad sensed there was something wrong. He stood up and walked over to the railings.

He cupped his hands over his mouth and shouted. "You okay?"

No response.

The pain from his legs had gone. He climbed over the bars and jumped down onto the marshland. Started running towards the person. The closer he got, the sharper his focus became. There was something familiar about the shape. The curve of the hips and the length of the arms.

"Molly?" He screamed at the top of his voice. "Molly."

She turned her head, the tufts of her hair pointing at the sky. Her expression was blank. Like she'd never seen him before in her life.

Brad's legs pumped hard.

At last, a glint of recognition in Molly's eyes.

He grabbed her around the waist. Lifted her from the ground. Kissed her face all over. Promised they would never be apart again.

forty six

Brad looked at the shape under the bedclothes. Traced the outline of her curves with his eyes. His desire was overwhelming. If he didn't get inside her he would burst. They had to find some privacy somehow. Time away from their son. Not easy when they were confined to barracks until the police activity died down.

Shem was busy drawing out a comic strip adventure on the hotel stationery.

The solution to the problem flashed into Brad's mind. "I'll get the bath on to get you warm and clean." Brad went into the bathroom. Put in the plug and turned on the taps.

"But I want to finish my story."

"Tell me what it's all about and then you can get in."

"It's about a super hero called Doolittle." He cuddled into his dad. "He turns into an animal when there's a problem."

"Great idea."

"So he changes into the best creature for the job."

Brad stared at the pictures. Saw the sea and a grey sausage with a fin on its back. "And in this one he's a shark."

"No, a dolphin." Of course. "Because there's a lady in trouble. She went for a long walk and the tide came in and she can't swim."

Shem must have picked up some of the conversation from their way to the hotel. "That's terrible."

"Not really. He has all the special powers he needs. Look."

Doolittle was flying through the air, the grinning woman holding on to the fin.

"That's amazing." It was. His son was a star. "Now tidy this up and get yourself ready. I'll make sure it's not too hot." He went through and gave the water a swirl. "It's perfect. You can turn it off when you're happy with it."

Shem stripped off, walked in a climbed into the bath. "Have we got any toys?"

Brad threw in a flannel, a bottle of shower gel and a canister of shaving cream. Left the room and closed the door.

He pressed his ear up against the wood. Heard the hissing of the foam and the splashing of childhood and knew he had bought enough time for what he intended.

He slipped off his shirt and trousers and slid under the duvet. Added another image to his scrapbook of memoires from the Northwood Hotel.

*

Four shopping trips. Four different supermarkets. One hell of a day.

There were plenty of provisions on board to last them for months. Tins of every kind. A spare room dedicated to carbohydrates. Bags of flour, bottles of long life, jars of sauces and jams for all occasions. There was ample water and juice just in case and enough chocolate to keep Charlie Bucket happy for a year.

The clothes selections were looking ahead to the autumn to come. Jumpers and fleeces and thermal wear. The sizing might be off and the fashion sense cutting a fine line, but they'd all be warm and contented with life whatever the weather threw their way.

Booze supplies were tiny. Brad figured it would do no harm to get their drinking under control for a while. He was almost looking forward to the challenge. To make up for it, he'd loaded up on box sets of DVDs, board games and books. They would never be bored on this voyage, of that he was certain.

Betsy's tanks were filled to capacity. Sixty gallons of red diesel, a hundred of water. There were spare cans of fuel for emergencies and two extra gas canisters for cooking to be on the safe side.

Duke had been kind enough to leave all the equipment in the galley and full sets of bedding for all the rooms. There were even oilskins for adults, so Brad had only had to buy waterproofs for Shem.

Brad ticked off each item on his list of essentials. The luxuries could wait until they stopped in Ireland.

The Shallows

All that remained was to lock up the boat and pray that he could smuggle his family through to the marina before the cops found them. Another small miracle would be needed for that to happen. He got down onto his knees and looked up towards the sky.

forty seven

Locke sipped at his second pint of lager of the evening. The beer garden of the Northwood was the perfect place to unwind. It seemed like the world had downed tools for a rest and stopped spinning for a while.

He was enjoying his time down south. The warm weather and the stone cottages suited him fine. It was like being on holiday without having to worry about the bills. Not that he had given up on the case. He just didn't want to make things move any faster than they had to. Shanks and Hawley would be out there working hard enough for all of them. They were the new breed. They'd learn to shift the gears as they gained experience. If they didn't, they'd end up burned out wrecks unfit for anything but dishing out parking tickets.

Locke sucked up the fresh air and cleared his mind. Wondered if they'd ever catch up with the Heaps. After all, some things just weren't meant to be. Take him and Doreen for example. She might have gone at sex like a grand prix driver, but these days Locke only really wanted a tour on a bus. He'd call it to a halt when he got home.

He took out a cigarette. Lit it and sucked hard. Knew immediately that it was one of the smokes he wouldn't enjoy. Took another drag anyway. He opened his notebook and flicked through to the most recently filled pages.

Underlined in capital letters, a question:
COULD THEY HAVE LEFT TOWN?

It was possible, but the evidence suggested otherwise. There were no trains entering Grange from the time she parked until the vehicle was found. As soon as they realised whose car it was, they positioned local officers at the station. Someone had been there for every departure since.

Leaving by road seemed just as unlikely. Surely they'd not have planned to leave their possessions behind. All except her handbag and the gun, that was. When the time came to close in, they would exercise plenty of caution. The navy boys were stationed nearby awaiting the call and the police had an armed squad on standby.

The Shallows

Molly and her son were still in Grange, Locke was sure of it. It was simply a matter of time before they got a sighting. There was no rush. As long as the powers that be were paying for his stay, the Heaps could take as long as they wanted to show themselves.

He swirled the dregs of his beer around in his glass and swallowed them down. He had a table for one booked at the Indian restaurant. Maybe the spices would inspire him. He stuffed his things into his pockets and was about to leave when a thought struck him. He wondered if anyone had bothered to check out this hotel. It was just the kind of place that could be overlooked. Grand. Imposing. The last place anyone would expect to find a runaway down on her luck.

Before leaving, he would go to the reception. See if they could shed any light on proceedings.

At the desk, the clerk was fiddling about on his phone. There was something wrong with his hand. A knot of scar tissue where his little finger should be. When he saw Locke approach, he put the phone down and straightened his jacket. "Good evening sir. How can I help?"

Locke took out his ID. Held it out and introduced himself. Picked up his bag and pulled out a cardboard file. "I was wondering if I could show you some photographs. In case you've seen any of the people I'm looking for."

"No problem." The guy studied the photos. Squinted when Locke flicked to the photo from the Eyemouth CCTV and pointed at Molly's face. "I know this lady. She was here a couple of days ago. With a kid."

"And you didn't think about reporting them to the police at the time?"

"You're kidding. The hairstyle may have been criminally awful, but it wasn't against the law."

Smartarse. "This happens to be a very dangerous woman. You may have had a lucky escape." Locke watched the smile disappear from the clerk's face. Enjoyed the moment. "I'd be grateful if you could tell me anything else."

"She had a kid with her."

Locke flicked further into the folder. Showed another photo. "This him?"

The clerk nodded.

"Did they book a room?"

The man laughed. "They aren't the type. The boy was asking about a man staying here."

"And you checked it out?"

"Pretended to. We're not allowed to give out the details of guests, but the child was so eager to find out that I had to do something."

"Did the guy he was looking for have a name?"

The receptionist tapped a pencil against his teeth. Clicked his fingers. "Collins. That was it." Didn't mean anything to Locke. "Easy to recall on account of the Apollo space mission."

"Nice work."

"It's nothing. They train you to remember names by association. Customers appreciate that, you see."

"He have a first name?"

"Ah. I'm not so good at that bit. We have no call to use them while we're working."

Locke flicked through the folder. Showed pictures of Brad Heap taken at his home and from the harbour. "I don't suppose this man is staying here."

The receptionist took a step back. "That's Mr Rudy Logue. Room 303. My, he was so much more handsome before he grew that beard, don't you think?"

Locke didn't give a shit. His mind was whirring. There was a lot to be done and he needed to find a place to start. He stroked his moustache and pondered the options.

Going to the room alone would be the quickest way to deal with this. It would also be the most stupid. What he required was the armed backup and a careful logistical assessment to ensure no innocents were hurt during the action.

"I'll need you to get the manager for me right away."

The Shallows

It looked as though Scotland's own Bonnie and Clyde were about to finish their journey. Locke hoped that their end would be nothing like the one in the movie. It was his job to make sure things went well. If shots were fired, he would consider the entire investigation to be a failure. Not even burying Red Fenton in a mountain of charges could sweeten that pill.

forty eight

"We've located Heap and his family sir." Shanks shuffled in circles as he spoke into the phone to the commander. "In Grange just as we expected."

"Excellent news. And you've sent in the team, I presume."

"Not yet. We're waiting for Inspector Locke to organise things with the hotel and to prepare his unit."

"You idiot." Briggs's voice was loud. Shanks pulled the receiver from his ear. "Remember what happened last time you left it to the civilians? It was a bloody fiasco. I'll not have you messing this one up for me."

The old bastard. It was always about him in the end. "It wouldn't look good if we undermined the police operation, sir. Especially when we may need to take the precaution of moving members of the public."

"You think I give a shit about protocol?" The voice got posher the angrier it became. "Look here, I don't care what Locke and his cronies think of us. I've got a minister breathing fire down my neck. Time isn't a luxury I possess."

"It won't be long. They're working on it."

"Damned right it won't. Get the unit in now. Let the dog see the rabbit."

"I can't see how we'll square that with our colleagues."

"Tell them it was crossed wires."

"But it was Locke who found Heap on both occasions. He deserves to lead the operation."

"Nonsense."

"And if anyone gets hurt."

"We'll put a spin on it that will screw with their brains."

Shanks paused. It was all wrong. Somehow he needed to change his boss's mind. "Could we wait until..."

"Get them in right now. That's an order."

"I don't think I can, sir."

"I wasn't asking."

"Then I'm afraid..."

"You realise the consequences of refusing a command?"

The Shallows

Shanks pressed the red button on his phone. Ended the conversation. Walked outside and daydreamed about what his new career might be.

forty nine

Brad paced up and down. He must have walked miles in the last hour, pacing the same section of carpet all the while.

Molly and Shem looked drugged. Their eyes were glazed with the boredom of waiting.

"Can't we go now Dad?" Shem's voice was flat.

"We need to hang on until dark."

"But that just gives them more time to find us."

"He's right, Brad." Molly sat up from the bed. Curled her arms around her legs. "What difference will a couple of hours make? I have to get out before I blow."

Brad was tired of arguing his case and his heart was with them both. He wanted nothing more than to put the whole episode behind them. Take off into the open water and head for freedom.

"Okay. We'll leave."

Shem jumped up from the bed. Bounced from the mattress and into his father's arms.

"There's just one thing I have to do before we go." Brad put his son down. Picked up an envelope from the pile on the table. "Find me a pen, Molly. This will only take a minute. Soon as I'm done here, we're off."

fifty

The corridor was silent. All the rooms had been checked and the residents had been taken downstairs.

Locke and Hawley stood behind their unit. The officers wore full protection and stood at either side of the room.

Locke received confirmation in his earpiece that the team outside were in position. He looked over at the sergeant leading the operation and nodded.

The sergeant turned the key, pushed open the door and the rest of his men disappeared into the room.

There was shouting and screaming and bangs galore. And then it went quiet. They'd managed to secure the area without a single shot being fired. Locke was finally able to breathe again. He patted Hawley on the shoulder and went inside.

fifty one

Captain Shanks stood at the top of the hill looking out across the bay. He was in no end of shit and yet he hadn't felt this calm for many years.

Down below, there was action in the car park. He noticed two adults and a child walking towards a Nissan Micra with tinted windows.

From this distance, he couldn't be sure, but they looked a hell of a lot like Brad, Molly and Shem Heap.

They filled the boot with bags, got inside and the lights came on.

Shanks froze. Knew he had to make a decision.

He could call it in. Remove his neck from the noose without breaking a sweat.

He watched the car as it pulled away. Thought about what Brad Heap had done to serve his country. About the voyages under the sea for months at a time. The way he tried to save Richardson. The courage he showed by visiting Richardson's family. None of those marked Heap as a coward. The guy was a hero. Things had gone astray for him that was all. He deserved an even break.

And Shanks was the man who was going to give it to him.

fifty two

The armed officers left the room with dejected expressions on their faces. All that adrenaline was still cranking up their bodies. It would take a good sergeant to defuse their energies before he sent them home. Locke recommended they go out and get shit-faced. That was what usually worked for him.

Locke and Hawley went inside. It was perfectly clean and tidy, as if ready for its next occupants.

Hawley pushed open the bathroom. Pulled the light cord and went inside.

Locke spotted an envelope on the bedside table. The message written on it read:

'For the cleaning staff.'

He picked it up and lifted the flap. Saw enough to make out a fifty pound note inside. Slipped it quickly into his pocket while he was still alone. He would decide later whether it was worth submitting as evidence.

fifty three

Brad stood in the wheelhouse and turned the key. The engine purred into action and the smell of diesel fumes filled the air.

Shem hadn't stopped running about the boat since they'd arrived. It was great to see that his enthusiasm for life hadn't diminished.

"Come here, Shem." Brad waved him over.

"What is it Dad?"

"I've got a little something for you." Brad took the chain from his neck and rubbed the crucifix. He held it out for Shem to take. "This is yours now, Shem. To bring you luck."

Shem looked up at his father. "I don't need it. I've got all the good fortune I need right here." He pointed to his heart, kissed Brad on the cheek and disappeared below deck.

Brad put the cross back on. Went around the boat and untied the ropes. Returned to the wheelhouse and sat on the captain's seat.

Molly walked in and passed over a cup of tea.

"Where we headed Skip?"

"To freedom, Mol."

She put her hand on his as he pushed the throttle forward.

"Or to Finland. Whichever we get to first."

He pulled her close. Turned the wheel. Drove the boat out of the harbour and steered the bow towards the moon.

If you have enjoyed this story, please consider taking a few moments to review the book and share your opinion.

Acknowledgements

With thanks, as ever, to Allan Guthrie for his encouragement, advice and selflessness. I'm ever grateful to him and to Kyle MacRae for having me over at Blasted Heath and giving me the confidence to carry on. A big thanks to Kath Middleton for her keen eye, her kindness and support. And to Tadg Farrington, a nod of appreciation for the weekly writing chats and his early viewing of The Shallows.

About The Author

Nigel Bird was born in Liverpool in the sixties, grew up in Preston, Lancashire and migrated south to study in London. During that time, he enjoyed many of the cultural benefits of the city and qualified as a primary school teacher. Among other things, he lived for several years on a narrow boat on the Regent's canal.

He moved to Scotland at the end of 1999 in the hope that he could begin the new century with a clean slate. He currently lives in Dunbar, on Scotland's east coast, with his wife and three children.

Nigel has been writing for many years. He co-edited the Rue Bella magazine between 1998 and 2003 with his brother, Geoff. He has won a number of small prizes for his poetry and short fiction and hopes that his longer work will be equally well-received one day.

He is the author of a number of short-story collections, novellas and novels including Southsiders, Mr Suit, Smoke and Dirty Old Town.

As well as writing, he continues to teach and is currently a Support for Learning teacher in Tranent.

**Published by Sea Minor 2016
copyright © 2016 Nigel Bird**

All rights reserved. No part of this publication may be reproduced or transmitted in any form or by any means without permission of the author. Nigel Bird has asserted his right under the Copyright, Designs and Patents Act 1988 to be identified as the author of this work.
Cover by Valdas Miskinis
All characters in this book are fictitious and any resemblance to actual persons, living or dead, is purely coincidental.

a Sea Minor Publication

© 2016

Printed in Great Britain
by Amazon